George Otto Trevelyan

The Ladies in Parliament and Other Pieces

George Otto Trevelyan

The Ladies in Parliament and Other Pieces

ISBN/EAN: 9783337154448

Printed in Europe, USA, Canada, Australia, Japan

Cover: Foto ©Andreas Hilbeck / pixelio.de

More available books at **www.hansebooks.com**

THE

LADIES IN PARLIAMENT

AND OTHER PIECES.

REPUBLISHED WITH ADDITIONS AND
ANNOTATIONS.

BY

G. O. TREVELYAN,

LATE SCHOLAR OF TRINITY COLLEGE, CAMBRIDGE, AND AUTHOR
OF THE "COMPETITION WALLAH."

CAMBRIDGE:
DEIGHTON, BELL, AND CO.
LONDON: BELL AND DALDY.
1869.

𝕮𝖆𝖒𝖇𝖗𝖎𝖉𝖌𝖊:

PRINTED BY J. PALMER.

PREFACE.

THE appearance of this little book is originally due to the demand which the commencement of each University year still brings with it for some Cambridge squibs published for the most part eleven years ago by a junior soph of Trinity College. The collection was taken in hand with the double purpose that those which are here inserted may be attainable in a convenient form, and that those which are omitted may perish utterly. Readers will excuse the ineffable youthfulness of productions written exclusively for the undergraduate market. The other pieces in the volume need, but cannot claim, the same indulgence.

October 1869.

CONTENTS.

LADIES IN PARLIAMENT.

B

THE LADIES IN PARLIAMENT.

A FRAGMENT AFTER THE MANNER OF AN OLD ATHENIAN COMEDY.

T HE LADIES IN PARLIAMENT was composed during
the great agitation which followed the rejection of
Mr. Gladstone's Reform Bill of 1866. The piece was at
first intended to be a modern and decent Ecclesiazusæ : not
such an imitation as would satisfy the scholar; but such as
would give to him who, for want of a better, goes by the name
of the general reader, some notion of how a Greek Comedian
might have written, when at his very worst, if he had lived
in the days of chignons and female suffrage. The idea of
producing something that should be Aristophanic from end
to end fell through; chiefly, no doubt, from the inability
of the author : but in part also because the simplicity which
is so quaint and pretty in Attic becomes childish in English.
Nor should it be forgotten that London society is too large
to admit that minuteness of allusion which was possible in
days when a small and highly cultivated community sup-

plied the poet with his materials and his audience. There is, however, one passage which reflects something of the old Greek manner; that namely which begins "We much revere our sires;" in which an attempt has been made to mimic the jovial conservatism which goes rollicking through the long swinging metres of Aristophanes. Care has like- wise been taken to preserve in these lines that utter con- tempt of dates, that highminded indifference to the unities of time, which he shares with every burlesque writer who is worth his salt. For instance, the old militia-men who have turned out to besiege Lysistrata and her accomplices repre- sent themselves as having taken part in ejecting Cleomenes, the Lacedæmonian king, from the Acropolis: an event which occurred ninety-nine years before the comedy was put upon the stage. "By Ceres," says one of them, "these women shall not laugh in my face : for Cleomenes, who was the first to try this game, did not go off without a flea in his ear; but with all his Spartan airs he had to lay down his arms, and march about his business with nothing but a little cape upon his shoulders, looking as if he had not washed or shaved for six years at least. So stoutly did I and my friends maintain the blockade, sleeping seven- teen deep before the gates of the citadel."

PLACE—*The South-east Angle of Berkeley Square.*

TIME—*A Morning in July*, 1866.

LADY SELINA.   LADY MATILDA.

Lady Selina.—'Tis hard upon ten.   Since a quarter to
   eight
I've paced up and down within sight of the gate.
If only you knew what a storm of abuse
Five minutes ago was prepared for your use !
But in your dear presence, I always have told you,
I can't find the heart or the language to scold you.
Well !   Now you are here, will you kindly explain
A question I frequently asked you in vain,
And tell me the cause of the constant depression
That weighs on your spirits this half of the session ?
You've not to my knowledge seen Phelps in *Macbeth*,
Nor suffered a recent bereavement by death :
From duns you're exempted : at doctors you scoff :
Your son has got in, and your girls are got off.
Then why are you silent, abstracted, and odd,
And deaf to a whisper, and blind to a nod ?
And when you are spoken to what makes you start ?
And why do you hum as if learning by heart,
Like members whom sometimes I watch in the parks
Rehearsing a string of impromptu remarks,
For which, in the course of a week, they intend
To beg of the House its indulgence to lend ?

Lady Matilda.—Selina ! The time has arrived to impart
The covert design of my passionate heart.
No vulgar solicitudes torture my breast.
No common ambition deprives me of rest.
'Tis not for a mind of my texture to fret
Though half Westbourne Terrace the *entrée* should get.
Unenvied, my rival may labour to deck
Her trumpery ball with a glimpse of Prince Teck.
My soul is absorbed in a scheme as sublime
As ever was carved on the tablets of time.
To-morrow, at latest, through London shall ring
The echo and crash of a notable thing.
I start from my fetters.   I scorn to be dumb.
Selina ! the Hour and the Woman are come.

    Unless I'm deceived, through the railings I spy
The form of a trusty and valiant ally.
'Tis young Mr. Gay.   Since at Brighton we met
He ranks as the leader and life of our set ;
For nothing, except what is useful, unfit ;
A dash of the poet, a touch of the wit.
A pet of the *salon*, the club, and the mess,
He knows he can write, and he thinks he can dress.
In Parliament, where he as yet is a dumb thing,
He sits for the Northern Division of something.
                                    [*Enter* Mr. GAY.
    Why, Charley, who ever would dream, I declare,
Of seeing your face at this hour in the square :—
Too late to be still on your way from a ball :
Too early for even an intimate call ?
And then so untidy !   I always can tell a
Preoccupied man by his tumbled umbrella.

And why is your brow with a shadow o'ercast?
And why did you stare on the ground as you passed
With one of those bits of white card in your mouth
Which gentlemen smoke who have been in the South?

Gay.—Dear ladies, be pleased to console with your
    pity
The slave of a tiresome election committee.
For this did I canvass, and promise, and flirt,
And drink so much sherry, and eat so much dirt?
For this my unfortunate sister persuade
To dress in a buff of most hideous shade
(Though yellow was just—the poor girl would object-
The very last tint that a blonde should select)?
For this did I pay in my Published Expenses
A sum which affected my guardian's senses:
And what in Unpublished I venture to own
To my Recognised Agent and banker alone?
For this did I stand on the hustings an hour,
My mouth full of egg, and my whiskers of flour,
Repeating in accents bewildered and hoarse
That sentence to which I have always recourse,
Whenever I come to the end of my tether,
About a strong pull and a pull altogether?—
In order to sulk on a quorum of five,
Attempting to keep my attention alive
By wondering wherefore the witnesses past
Should each be more dirty and drunk than the last,
And whether the next one can possibly swear
To cooler untruths than the man in the chair:
While over the window-sill temptingly play
The blithe mocking beams of the beautiful day,

Which shine on the Row, where in maidenly pride
She dashes along at her chaperon's side !
Her tresses——

Lady Matilda.—Excuse me.   We have not to spare
The time to descant on her ladyship's hair.
The moment has come for the metre to change :
Since prudent stage-managers always arrange
At this point of the piece that the music should play,
For fear of impatient spectators, who say :
" These folks with their prologue are likely to bore
     us.
Let's take a short nap, and wake up for the chorus."

[*Sings.*]—As towards the City on the Shoreditch side
     Above a dreary waste of tiles we glide,
     Rejoicing that the Eastern Coast Express
     For once has brought us home in time to dress,
     Pale with the day-long labours of the woof
          We see the weavers from their garrets crawl
     To court the air of evening on the roof,
          And their trained flocks of tumblers round them
               call :—
               So I must modulate my throat,
               And pitch a high and jocund note,
               With melody the town to fill
               From Regent's Park to Campden Hill,
               And bid the doves together hurry
               Who get their plumes from Mistress Murray :
               Though certain little pigeons blue
               Prefer the feathers of Descou.

Haste to my aid, nor deem the summons pert,
 Ye stately queens of fashion and of fame
Whose palaces in fair succession skirt
 The park which from its colour takes a name :
And ye who dwell in Hill Street's ancient halls,
 Where o'er the porch, whose oil-lamp faintly winks,
A rusted quaint extinguisher recalls
 The bygone days of chairmen and of links ;
Or 'midst the pleasant back streets of the West
 That lurk 'twixt Grosvenor and Cadogan Place,
Where newly-married couples choose a nest,
 And with the wedding-gifts their drawing-room grace ;
Or where, remote from senate and from court,
 In vistas white of never-ending squares,
The pensioned Indian's undisturbed resort,
 Far towards the setting sun Tyburnia's stucco glares

Hither to the rescue, ladies !
 Let not fear your spirits vex.
On the plan by me that made is
 Hangs the future of our sex.
No despised or feeble sister
 Bids you rally for the strife.
This is one who never missed her
 Opportunities in life :—
Who with no misplaced ambition
 Has her social flag unfurled,
And attained the proud position
 Of a woman of the world.

Shall she, then, be left to mourn her
    Isolation and her shame?
Come in troops round Hyde Park Corner,
    Every true Belgravian dame.
Don a light and simple toilette :
    Or, if any doubt you feel
Lest the morning glare should soil it,
    Come, O come, in déshabille !

For the town is just awaking,
    And you will not meet a soul,
Save, perhaps, Lord Chelmsford taking
    His accustomed morning stroll ;
Or some swells who've chanced to linger
    Over their cigars and chats,
Twirling latch-keys round their finger
    As they loiter home from Pratt's.*

Keep the route of Piccadilly, when your expedition starts :
Though the way be somewhat hilly, and the crossings swarm
        with carts.
There on warm mid-season Sundays Fryston's bard is pleased
        to wend,
Whom the Ridings trust and honour, freedom's staunch and
        genial friend,
Known where shrewd hard-handed craftsmen cluster round
        the Northern kilns—
He whom men style Baron Houghton, but the gods call
        Dicky Milnes.

* A fashionable evening club in the vicinity of Brookes's.

Lo ! the Duke with outstretched truncheon indicates your
line of march,
Motioning " Up, girls, and at 'em !" from the summit of his
arch.
Follow that luxurious pavement all along the Dandy's slope :
Past the spot where Tom and Jerry robbed the door of Mr.
Hope :*
(May they sink in outer darkness for their sacrilegious
loot,
Just as his Italian marbles fade beneath the London soot !)
Past the wall which screens the mansion, hallowed by a
mighty shade,†
Where the cards were cut and shuffled when the game of
state was played.
Now in those world-noted chambers subalterns exchange
cheroots,
And with not ill-natured banter criticise each other's boots ;
And a knot of young lieutenants at their new club entrance
lean
Little recking of the heroes who have stepped those gates
between.
Then in front of Francatelli's, where men never seem to know
Whether they may take their sisters, turning towards the left
you go ;
And in picking out the foot-track see that special care you
use,
Since the lane down which you walk is half a street and half
a mews.

---

* The reader may remember that a valuable knocker, which, with
equal taste and public spirit, Mr. Hope had placed upon his door in
Piccadilly, was some years ago abstracted by the Mohawks of the period.
† Cambridge House is now the Naval and Military Club.

Stay not till you reach the kerb-stone, where in Berkeley
 Square I stand,
With the princely house of Lansdowne and an ice-shop on
 each hand,
(Overlook a slip of grammar sanctified by Byron's pen,)
Thinking out our liberation from the irksome rule of men;
Peering back towards Lady Jersey's; twirling the expectant
 thumb.
By our common hopes and fortunes I adjure you.   Sisters;
 come.

     Enter a number of Ladies.

Gay.—No passing whim, no crotchet vain and light,
 Has snatched you, ladies, from your *Morning Post*,
Whose columns with their tale of over-night
 Give relish to a tiny plate of toast.
The hour is ripe an evil to debate
 Which threatens over head and ears to souse
In seas of trouble this afflicted state——

Lady Matilda.—I think we're just enough to form a
 House,
And, as for Speaker, I have seldom seen a
More proper person than our friend Selina.
You, Charley, fetch the roller from the square,
And prop it up to represent her Chair.
Some pebbles underneath will keep it steady.

Gay.—But where's the Wig?

Lady Matilda.—She's got one on already.
I'll take my station on the fountain's base,
Which kind Lord Lansdowne gave our square to grace:

And when I think to whom my seat I owe
I hope in eloquence to match with Lowe.
The ministry, as decent is and fit,
Shall just in front along the pavement sit,
And try to look as if they did not mind
The buffets which assail them from behind.
We'll name a sensible and pleasant madam
To act for Brand, and some smart girl for Adam;
Who, when the younger members steal away
    To try the croquet hoops, or eat an ice,
    Shall seize their skirts, and stop them in a trice,
And bid them either pair at once or stay.

1st Lady.—As from her agitation I imply
Matilda means to catch the Speaker's eye.
We used to notice, while together waiting
Behind the bars of Lord Charles Russell's grating,
That on the verge of any fine display
Men twist their feet in that uneasy way.

2nd Lady.—She's rising now, and taking off her bonnet,
And probably will end by sitting on it.
For oft, as sad experiences teach,
The novice, trembling from his maiden speech,
Drops flustered in his place, and crushes flat
His innocent and all-unconscious hat.
And my poor husband spoiled an evening suit
By plumping down amidst a heap of fruit
Which some admiring friend, his thirst to quench,
Had peeled beside him on the Treasury Bench.

Lady Matilda.—Since Britain first, to hear her charter
      sung
In florid numbers by angelic tongue,
At heaven's injunction left the azure deep :
Since acres, kine, and tenements, and sheep
Enrich the eldest, while the younger sons
Monopolize the talents and the duns :—
Since pretty Phillis first began to hook
Reluctant shepherds with her maiden crook,
By female instinct taught to spurn the notes
Of Strephon's pipe for Damon's vine and goats :—
In every age, so rule the Powers above,
Maternal foresight makes a toil of love ;
From past repulses learns that all in vain
The net is spread in sight of any swain ;
And wins an up-hill battle, foot by foot,
From Introduction on to Question put.

I seek not then your conscience to perplex
With strictures on the mission of our sex.
No London mother ever yet repined
Beneath a burden shared by all her kind.
In one short line my grievance thus I state :—
Our youngest girls come out a year too late.
For in the days when Pam retained the wheel
We knew the men with whom we had to deal.   [*Applause.*
Then sucking statesmen seldom failed in seeing
The final cause and import of their being.
They dressed ; they drove a drag ; nor sought to shirk
Their portion of the matrimonial work.
They flocked to rout and drum by tens and twelves ;
Danced every dance ; and left their cards themselves,

While some obliging senatorial fag
Slipped their petitions in the Speaker's bag.
They charged their colleagues of maturer ages
With pushing local bills through all their stages ;
Consigned the dry routine of public life
To legislators furnished with a wife ;
And thought it much if once in twenty nights
They sauntered down to swell the party fights.

But now what fond regrets pervade my breast
To note a stripling, from some lofty nest
Of bright historic fame but lately fledged ;
To no loved object, save the ballot, pledged ;
By travel taught less sharply to recoil
From notions grown on Transatlantic soil ;
Weaned from the creed of all his kin and kith ;
On Bentham nursed, and fed on Goldwin Smith ;
And fresh from learning at the feet of Grote
How governors should rule and freemen vote ;
His one supreme intent, through woe and weal,
To hold by Gladstone as *he* held by Peel.
Refined yet negligent ; for want of taste
In every groom's and valet's eyes disgraced ;
Scorned by his tailor ; little apt to mind
Though fashion leave him half a year behind.
In social wiles unversed, a rumoured ball
Extracts from him no mild suggestive call :
Nor deigns he in the ranged quadrille to stand,
Unless to claim a fair constituent's hand
Or serve some party end ; and, if by chance
On one of our dear girls he wastes a dance,

She hears him wonder, 'midst the figure's pause,
How Coleridge will dispose of Heathcote's clause :
Dread words, which damp, beyond all power to scorch,
The match that might have kindled Hymen's torch.

And when at noon along the joyous Row
The ceaseless streams of youth and beauty flow,
Though azure habit and artistic hat
Invite to snatches of half-tender chat,
He turns where, grave and silent, yet serene,
His chieftain rides two mirthful troops between,
And meets the kindly breeze that fans away
Each trace and relic of the nightly fray ;—
The trifling slip, by eloquence retrieved ;—
The words misconstrued, purpose misconceived ;—
The forced and mocking laugh of feigned surprise
That down the hostile lines by concert flies ;—
The taunt of fear too fevered to be just,
And shallowness which deems itself mistrust ;—
The venomed stab of envy, that would fain
Assume the mien and language of disdain.

Yet long we suffered, chastened to endure
The ills that picnics and July might cure.
But summer wanes, and visions once so fair
Result in Prorogation and despair.
The mother sees a wan and jaded band
Unwed, undanced-with, and untalked-to, stand.
The wife, beguiled by dim and flickering hopes
Of random callers, in her boudoir mopes,
Or sits, with ears intent on casual knocks,
Though Patti sings, sole inmate of her box.

1st Lady.—Yes, indeed! 'Tis past all bearing, when a
husband slights his bride
Who last Christmas still was blushing at her elder sister's
side;
Still on some minute allowance finding collars, boots, and
gloves;
Still to cousinly flirtations limiting her list of loves;
Still by stern domestic edict charged on no account to read
Any of Miss Brontë's novels, or to finish *Adam Bede.*
When she says to Charles or Henry: "Will you take me
out a walk?
Since the Bill is in Committee scarcely find we time to talk;
And to-day I can't go shopping, though I have so much
to do,
For the gray you bought in Yorkshire always seems to cast
a shoe.
Quite the nicest way to spend a penny is to hire a chair,
And from underneath the lime-trees watch Lord Granville
drive his pair.
We may catch a look at Arthur, struggling with his team of
roans:
And I'm told he soon will break his own or some one else's
bones,
Since he's not what fast young ladies prone to slang would
call a dab.
Then we'll dine, and run together in a cosy hansom cab
To the Prince of Wales's playhouse, though it be not quite
the thing,
For my heart is set on hearing pretty Fanny Josephs sing.
You shall have the soup I copied from the Windham Club
receipt,
(Though papa declared on Sunday that it was not fit to eat,)

Followed by those salmon cutlets which the cook has learned
    to do,
And perhaps a little turbot, just enough for me and you."

  But the budding politician " Not to-night, my pet," re-
    plies ;
" I've a motion on the paper, and must wait my time to rise ;
Since in this distracting crisis ill the private member fares,
If he be not Bright or Kinglake, should he miss his place at
    prayers.
You may ask the girls to dinner,—add the urn, and call it
    tea.
Well I know the ways of women when they get an evening
    free !
We shall sit with ranks unbroken, cheering on the fierce
    debate,
Till the sun will light me homewards as I trudge through
    Storey's Gate
Racked with headache, pale, and haggard, worn by nights
    of endless talk,
While the early sparrows twitter all along the Birdcage Walk.
O, to roam o'er glen and corrie, far away from fuss and
    sham,
Lunching on a chicken sandwich and a slice of bread and
    jam,
Tramping after grouse or partridge through the soft Sep-
    tember air,
Both my pockets stuffed with cartridge, and my heart devoid
    of care !"

  Gay.—If Ministers wish us the Tories to beat,
  They surely should grant us the leisure to eat :

But Liberal youngsters do nothing but fast
Since ever this measure began to be passed.
Brand kept me from table three nights in one week
By hinting that Lowe was intending to speak ;
Although I suspect to detain me he tried,
In case Captain Hayter thought fit to divide.
When all that is clever at Arthur's or White's
Has set itself down for the gayest of nights ;—
When the steward is warned, and the cook has a hint
To see there be neither redundance nor stint,
That the whitebait are crisp, and the curry is hot,
Since some one is coming who knows what is what ;—
When winecups all mantling with ruby are seen,
(Whatever the mantling of winecups may mean) ;—
When over the port of the innermost bin
The circle of diners are laughing with Phinn ;—
When Brookfield has hit on his happiest vein,
And Harcourt is capping the jokes of Delane ;—
Possessed by alarm of impending collisions
With doubtful supporters who count my divisions
I crouch 'neath the gallery eating my fill
Of biscuits concealed in the folds of a Bill :
While stretched at my feet a promiscuous heap
Of gentlemen lie in the gangway asleep.

Lady Matilda.—One chance remains, the last and surest
    course
Of injured worth :—a bold appeal to force.
Through crescent, terrace, circus, and arcade
Shall scouts proclaim a feminine crusade.
Let Knightsbridge, Pimlico, and Brompton meet,
Where Grosvenor Place is lost in Eaton Street ;

While Portman Square and Hyde Park Gardens march
At break of dawn beneath the Marble Arch.
Across Victoria Road, with beat of drum,
Straight towards the Abbey bid our musters come ;
Beset the House, and all approaches guard
From furthest Millbank round to Palace Yard ;
Invest the lobbies ; raise across the courts
A barricade of Bluebooks and Reports ;
Suspend for good the Orders of the Day ;
To serve as hostage seize Sir Thomas May ;
And with one daring stroke for ever close
The fount and origin of these our woes.
Till man, who holds so light our proper charms,
Is brought to reason by material arms,
And learns afresh, what all his fathers knew,
His highest function, our most cherished due. [*Applause.*

    2nd Lady.—Thus we sit our treason netting,
      Talking words that might have hung us,
    All the while like geese forgetting
      We have here an Owl among us.*
        [*They surround* GAY *in a threatening attitude.*

Lady Matilda.—The Whig profane who rudely pries
    In regions masked from vulgar eyes,—
    Who once has trod the sacred rug
    Where Tories lounge in conclave snug,
    And listen while their whips recite
    The tactics of a coming fight,
    Or speculate in murmurs low
    How far the Cave intends to go,—

---

* The *Owl* was then in its third season of publication.

That rash intrusive wasp alive
Will never quit the Carlton hive.
We, less severe, accord you leave
To earn an undeserved reprieve
By coaxing with harmonious call
Your vagrant brethren hither all,
And warning them in silence deep
Our counsels and resolves to keep.

Gay [*sings.*]—Gentle birds of plumage tawny,
 Whom the pale policeman greets
Flitting nestwards, as at dawn he
 Treads his weary round of streets;
Tribe vivacious, bound to serve a
Term of seasons to Minerva;
This a poet, that a sceptic;
 Tufted some, and others crestless;
Roguish, easy, gay, eupeptic,
 Frisky, truant, vague, and restless;
Haunt and perch for ever changing
 As the needs of gossip call;
Towards the hour of luncheon ranging
 Round the board-rooms of Whitehall,
Where a busy race of men
Tie the tape and drive the pen,
Till the welcome stroke of four
Open throws their office door.
There the food which suits his humour
 Never yet an Owl has lacked:
Scraps of talk and crumbs of rumour,
 Here a guess, and there a fact.

So, through each Department hopping,
Culling truth, and fiction dropping,
　　Off you fly to print and risk it,
When your crop with news is stored
By some lazy junior lord
　　Yawning o'er his mid-day biscuit.

Tu-whit! Tu-whoo! Tu-whit! Tu-whoo!
　　When the warning note I utter
All the tuneful, roving crew
　　Round their mate will swiftly flutter.

Once again, when chill and dark
Twilight thins the swarming park,
Bearing home his social gleaning,
Jests and riddles fraught with meaning,
Scandals, anecdotes, reports,
Seeks the fowl a maze of courts
Which with aspect towards the west
　　Fringe the street of sainted James,
Where a warm secluded nest
　　As his sole domain he claims;
From his wing a feather draws,
　　Shapes for use a dainty nib,
　　Pens his parody or squib,
Combs his down, and trims his claws,
And repairs where windows bright
Flood the sleepless square with light;
Where behind the tables stand
Gunter's deaf and voiceless band;
Where his own persuasive hoot
Mingles with the strains of Coote,

The Ladies in Parliament.

While, retiring and advancing,
  Softly through the music's storm
Timid girls discourse on dancing,
  And are mute about Reform ;
In a sea of flounces swimming ;
  Waves of rustling tulle above ;
Strewn below the wrecks of trimming,
  Shattered fan and crumpled glove.

Tu-whit ! Tu-whoo ! Tu-whit ! Tu-whoo !
  When they see I'm of a feather
All the tuneful, roving crew
  Speedily will flock together.

Enter Chorus of Owls.

Chorus.—What the dickens means our brother
  By tu-whitting and tu-whooing ?
Much we fear he's laid another
  Pun, as he is always doing ;
Or has hatched a long acrostic
  From the dictionary taken ;
Something fit to pose a Gnostic,
  And defy the skill of Bacon.

But now for half-an-hour must cease
The plot and business of the piece :
Because the audience has been
Long anxious for a change of scene,
In dread of getting, ere it budges,
As old as Derby's Irish judges.
So shift the canvass, while we speak
A chorus modelled from the Greek.

We much revere our sires, who were a mighty race of men.*

For every glass of port we drink they nothing thought of
ten.

They dwelt above the foulest drains.   They breathed the
closest air.

They had their yearly twinge of gout, and little seemed to
care.

They set those meddling people down for Jacobins or fools

Who talked of public libraries, and grants to normal schools ;

Since common folks who read, and write, and like their
betters speak,

Want something more than pipes, and beer, and sermons
once a week.

And therefore both by land and sea their match they rarely
met,

But made the name of Britain great, and ran her deep in debt.

They seldom stopped to count the foe, nor sum the moneys
spent,

But clenched their teeth and straight ahead with sword and
musket went.

And, though they thought if trade were free that England
ne'er would thrive,

They freely gave their blood for Moore, and Wellington, and
Clive.

And, though they burned their coal at home, nor fetched
their ice from Wenham,

They played the man before Quebec and stormed the lines
at Blenheim.

---

* εὐλογῆσαι βουλόμεσθα τοὺς πατέρας ἡμῶν, ὅτι
ἄνδρες ἦσαν τῆσδε τῆς γῆς ἄξιοι, καὶ τοῦ πέπλου. κ.τ.λ.
Knights, 565.

When sailors lived on mouldy bread, and lumps of rusty pork,
No Frenchman dared his nose to shew between the Downs
    and Cork;
But now that Jack gets beef and greens, and next his skin
    wears flannel,
The *Standard* says we've not a ship in plight to keep the
    Channel.

And, while they held their own in war, our fathers shewed
    no stint
Of fire, and nerve, and vigour rough, whene'er they took to
    print.
They charged at hazard through the crowd, and recked not
    whom they hurt,
And taught their Pegasus to kick and splash about the dirt;
And every jolly Whig who drank at Brookes's joined to goad
That poor young Heaven-born Minister with epigram and
    ode,
Because he would not call a main, nor shake the midnight box,
Nor flirt with all the pretty girls like gallant Charley Fox.
But now the press has squeamish grown, and thinks in-
    vective rash;
And telling hits no longer lurk 'neath asterisk and dash;
And poets deal in epithets as soft as skeins of silk,
Nor dream of calling silly lords a curd of ass's milk.
And satirists confine their art to cutting jokes on Beales,
Or snap like angry puppies round a mightier tribune's heels:
Discussing whether he can scan and understand the lines
About the wooden Horse of Troy,* and when and where he
    dines:

---

* This animal played almost as prominent a part in the overthrow
of Lord Russell's administration as in the capture of Pergamus.

Though gentlemen should blush to talk as if they cared a
    button
Because one night in Chesham Place he ate his slice of
    mutton.

Since ever party strife began the world is still the same,
And Radicals from age to age are held the fairest game.
E'en thus the Prince of Attic drolls, who dearly loved to sup
With those who gave the fattest eels and choicest Samian
    cup,
Expended his immortal fun on that unhappy tanner
Who twenty centuries ago was waving Gladstone's banner :
And in the troubled days of Rome each curled and scented
    jackass
Who lounged along the Sacred Way heehawed at Caius
    Gracchus,
And vented calumnies as coarse, and impudent, and thorough
As any noisy barrister who fights a Surrey borough.*
So now all paltry jesters run their maiden wit to flesh on
A block of rugged Saxon oak, that shews no light impression ;
At which whoe'er aspires to chop had better guard his eye,
And towards the nearest cover bolt, if once the splinters fly.

Then surely it were best to drop an over-worried bone,
And, if we've nothing new to say, just let the League alone ;

* "Has Mr. Bright ever stood for Rochdale? Dare he ever stand
for it? Not he! He has been hooted away from his own premises.
His own people distrust him. What did he do in the cotton famine?
I will tell you what he did. He wanted to give the workpeople a loan
that was to be repaid in so many years, so that during those years he
would have these people as his serfs at his beck and call, to do what he
pleased with, and to prevent their rising when he chose to put wages at
whatever rate he liked?"

Or work another vein, and quiz those patrons of their race
Who like the honest working-man, but like him in his
    place ;—
Who bid us mark that artisans their apathy display,
And prove how cheaply they regard the question of the day,
By forming little groups of which some four would make a
    million
To stare at Colonel Dickson perched behind a blue postilion ;—
Who, proud of rivalling the pig which started for Dundalk
Because it thought that Paddy wished towards Carlingford
    to walk,
In slavish contradiction all their private judgment smother,
And blindly take one course because John Bright prefers
    another.

Let's rather speak of what was felt by us who value "Yeast"
On learning who had led the choir at that triumphal feast
Where Hampshire's town and county joined a civic wreath
    to fling
O'er him, the great proconsul, whose renown through time
    shall ring
In deathless cadence borne along pianoforte wires,
As memories heroic haunt the chords of Grecian lyres.
That he, who gave our ancient creeds their first and rudest
    shock,
Till half the lads for pattern took his Chartist Alton Locke,
Should tell us that Debrett within his gilded leaves contains
The virtue of the British isles, the beauty, and the brains !*

---

* At the banquet given to Governor Eyre at Southampton Dr.
Kingsley is reported to have said that the House of Lords contained all
the genius and all the virtue of the country, and that it was rapidly
monopolising all the beauty :—likewise that the conduct of Eyre in
Jamaica was a brilliant manifestation of "modern chivalry."

As if all moral folks were peers !   As if the sweetest kisses
Had ceased to lurk between the lips of many a charming missis !
While Cobden and Carlyle can boast no tall heraldic tree,
And Tennyson is still Esquire, and Mill a plain M.P.
That he, whose brave old English tale set all our veins aglow,
(How Hawkins, Cavendish, and Drake, went sailing West-
          ward Ho,
And how they led the Dons a life, and fought them man to man,
And spared them when they begged for grace, and chased
          them when they ran,)
Should teach that "modern chivalry" has found its noblest
          egress
In burning Baptist villages, and stringing up a negress !*

But 'tis not on topics like those
      Their talent that owls should exhibit.
More suited for vultures and crows
      Are puffs of the cat and the gibbet.
We leave it for Newman to search
      The doctrine professed by a parson
Who runs from his schools and his church
      To gloat upon hanging and arson.
Like garrulous birds we resort
      In quest of a frolicsome theme
Where butterflies quarrel and sport
      On the brink of Society's stream.

* We once could say with pride that no woman had been put to
death by Englishmen for a political offence since the days of Judge
Jeffreys. It was reserved for modern chivalry in the year of grace 1865
to hang three women on the charge of rebellion, unaccompanied by
murder: besides Rosa Macbean, who was shot "by soldiers without
trial," and a woman, "name unknown," hung by a Court Martial which
did business on the principle of "proceedings not kept": gallant and
gentle feats duly chronicled in the Appendix to the Report of the Royal
Commission, pp. 1135, 1136, 1137, and 1142.

Then hither and listen, whoever
　　Would learn in our pages the miracle
Of passing for witty and clever
　　Without being voted satirical !
He'd better be apt with his pen
　　Than well-dressed and well-booted and gloved
Who likes to be liked by the men,
　　By the women who loves to be loved :
And Fashion full often has paid
　　Her good word in return for a gay word,
For a song in the manner of Praed,
　　Or an anecdote worthy of Hayward.

And hither, you sweet schoolroom beauties,
　　Who only at Easter came out !
We'll teach you your dear little duties
　　At ball-room, and concert, and rout.
With whom you may go down to supper ;
　　And where you can venture to please ;
And what you should say about Tupper,
　　And what of the cattle disease ;
And when you must ask a new member
　　Why *he* did not move the Address,
And hint how you laughed last November
　　On reading his squibs in the Press.

You Pitts of the future, we'll get you
　　To shew yourselves modest and smart,
And, if you speak hastily, set you
　　Three pages of Hansard by heart.

Whenever with quoting you bore us
    (As pert young Harrovians will)
Your last repetition from Horace,
    You'll write out a chapter of Mill.
But if you can think of a hit
    That's brilliant and not very blue
We'll greet it by piping " Tu-whit,"
    And mark it by hooting " Tu-whoo."

So scorn not to heed our advice,
    Nor deem us impertinent fowls,
Nor say that the catching of mice
    Is the proper department for Owls :
For Palmerston liked us and read us,
    And all the vicinity knew
That the ivy which sheltered and bred us
    Around the old forest-king grew.
Though parties and principles perish,
    Though faint is consistency's flame,
Our loyalty ever shall cherish
    That loved and illustrious name.

Just one-and-fifty* years had gone since on the Belgian
    plain
Amidst the scorched and trampled rye Napoleon turned his
    rein,
And once again in panic fled a gallant host and proud,
And once again a chief of might 'neath Fortune's malice
    bowed.

---

* On the 18th June, 1866, the Liberal Government was defeated
upon Lord Dunkellin's Amendment ;—defeat that was followed by
resignation.

So vast and serried an array, so brave and fair to view,
Ne'er mustered yet around the flag of mingled buff and
blue,—
So potent in the show of strength, in seeming zeal so bold,—
Since Grey went forth in 'Thirty-two to storm Corruption's
hold.
But in the pageant all is bright, and, till the shock we feel,
We learn not what is burnished tin, and what is tempered
steel.
When comes the push of charging ranks, when spear and
buckler clash,
Then snaps the shaft of treacherous fir, then holds the
trusty ash.
And well the fatal truth we knew when sounds of lawless fight
In baleful concert down the line came pealing from our
right,
Which in the hour of sorest need upon our centre fell,
Where march the good old houses still that love the people
well.
As to and fro our battle swayed in terror, doubt, and shame,
Like wolves among the trembling flock the Tory vanguard
came,
And scattered us as startled girls to tree and archway go
Whene'er the pattering hailstorm sweeps along the crowded
Row.
A moment yet with shivered blade, torn scarf, and pennon
reft
Imperial Gladstone turned to bay amidst our farthest left,
Where, shoulder tight to shoulder set, fought on in sullen
pride
The veterans staunch who drink the streams of Tyne, and
Wear, and Clyde ;

Who've borne the toil, and heat, and blows of many an
    hopeless fray;
Who serve uncheered by rank and fame, unbought by place
    or pay.
At length, deserted and outmatched, by fruitless efforts spent
From that disastrous field of strife our steps we homeward
    bent,
Erelong to ride in triumph back, escorted near and far
By eager millions surging on behind our hero's car;
While blue and yellow streamers deck each Tory convert's
    brow,
And both the Carltons swell the shout : " We're all Reformers
    now !"

HORACE AT THE UNIVERSITY OF ATHENS.

D

HORACE AT THE UNIVERSITY OF ATHENS.

THIS little extravaganza is at the diadvantage of having been composed for acting, and altered for printing. It lays claim, however, to perfect historical accuracy; as it faithfully records the known occurrences in the life of Horace; his residence at Athens as a student; his enlistment in the republican army; his behaviour at Philippi; his pardon at the instance of Mæcenas; and his appointment to a post in the Roman Treasury. That it is accepted by undergraduates as a fair representation of undergraduate life and thought is testified by the local demand having brought it through three editions. The passages that refer to the fighting then taking place in Virginia will serve as specimens of the tone in which young Englishmen of the day wrote and talked about the greatest event of our time.

Dramatis Personæ.

AUGUSTUS.
MÆCENAS.
BRUTUS.
CASSIUS.

CAIUS,
BALBUS,
HORACE,   *Students of the University*
DECIUS MUS,   *of Athens.*
SEMPRONIUS VIRIDIS, *a Freshman,*

THE VICE-CHANCELLOR OF THE UNIVERSITY.
THE PUBLIC ORATOR.
QUINTUS RUSSELLUS MAXIMUS, *the Special Correspondent of the*
    "Acta Diurna."
THE GHOST OF CÆSAR.
LYDIA.
STUDENTS, SOLDIERS, GUARDS, &C.

SCENE I.

In front of the great gate of the College.   Lydia's *house on the left of the stage.*

Caius *and* Balbus *in cap and gown.*   Horace *lounging in the back-ground.*

Caius.—What time d'ye call it, Balbus?   Why, good
     heaven,
I do declare it's only half-past seven !
And I was up last night till after two,
And lost—the Furies know how much—at loo.
As I was dreaming how you trumped my knave
The bell its matutinal warning gave :
Forth from his cosy bed the student shoots
Clad in a toga and a pair of boots,
Knocks down his soap-dish, blunders with his brushes,
And, half-undressed, to morning temple rushes.
     Balbus.—Caius, my worthy comrade—
     Cai.—   If you please
I very much prefer to be called Keys.
     Bal.—Well : who's that young Apulian ? To my know-
     ledge
I was on nodding terms with all the college.
     Cai.—That ? Why, 'tis little Horace. Don't you know
     him ?
The same that got the Chancellor's Prize Poem ;
Who wears six rings, and curly as a maid is ;
Who's always humming songs about the ladies ;

Who never comes inside the gates till four;
Who painted green the Senior Tutor's door.
I'll make you both acquainted.   Here, my fuchsia,
This is the famous freshman from Venusia.
And this is Balbus, cleverest of dabs
At losing pewters and at catching crabs.
As to his antecedents, you must look
In the first page of Henry's Latin Book.
    Hor.—Can this be Balbus, household word to all,
Whose earliest exploit was to build a wall?
Who, with a frankness that I'm sure must charm ye,
Declared it was all over with the army.
Can this be he who feasted, as 'twas said,
The town at fifty sesterces a-head?
But, while the thankless mob his bounty quaffed,
Historians add—that there were some who laughed.
I should be deeply honoured if I might
Secure your presence at my rooms to-night.
A friend has sent me half-a-dozen brace
Of thrush and blackbird from a moor in Thrace.
These we will have for supper, with a dish
Of lobster-patties, and a cuttle-fish;
While those who have not dined in hall may rally O
Round that gigantic mess beginning galeo—
Lepado—temacho—and the Lord knows what.
You'll find it all in Liddell and in Scott.
    Bal.—A thousand thanks: the honour will be mine.
But our Dynamic lecture stands for nine.
Let's go to breakfast, Caius: since I hate
To scald my mouth for fear of being late.
                [*Exeunt all but* Horace *and* Decius Mus.
    Hor.—My Decius, since our earliest private school
You always were my fond and faithful fool.

I eat the blackberries : you scratched your legs.
I took the nests : you blew the addled eggs.
When we stole out at night to see the play
'Twas you, not I, who could not sit next day.
And now we live, a pair of trusty friends,
With common pleasures and with common ends.
To you, my Decius Mus, to you alone
I trust the secret that I burn to own.
Why is my colour gone, my visage lank ?
Why did I steer our boat against the bank ?
Why is my wine untasted in the glass ?
Why do I tremble when the proctors pass ?
By Proserpine below, by Jove above,
By mine own head I swear that I'm in love !

    Dec. M.—Don't swear so loud. I've not the slightest
      doubt of it.
I never knew the time when you were out of it.
    Hor.—'Tis true ! 'Tis true ! But this is not the same.
So pure, so ardent, and so bright a flame !
Oh face ! oh form celestial !
    Dec. M.—   I knows her.
Quis multâ gracilis te, Pyrrha, in rosâ ?
    Hor.—Pyrrha, the faithless sorceress !
    Dec. M.—   Ah, I see !
Extremum Tanaim si biberes, Lyce.
Or her you told us of last night when beery,—
Die et argutâ properet Neœræ.
    Hor.—My sweetheart, Mus, outshines Neœra far
As D'Orsey's comet* beats the polar star.

---

* In the year 1860 the Rev. Mr. D'Orsey obtained the Chancellor's
medal for a poem on the Great Comet of 1858. This gentleman soon
after became English lecturer at Corpus College, and commenced a

Unkind as Lyce, and than Pyrrha giddier,
Whom can I mean but lovely lively Lydia?
  Dec. M. [*aside*]—Perdition catch this fellow and his
    curls !
That such a doll as this should please the girls !
Lydia, my fondest hope, my only joy !
[*Aloud*] Horace, you're taken in this time, my boy !
Your darling Lydia is not all you think.
For a young lady she's a whale at drink :
And, though I don't believe the fact the least,
They say she went to the Olympian feast
In young Muræna's drag.
  Hor.—   They lie—they lie !
They dared not breathe a word if I were by.
I love her, though she's petulant and cruel,
As Radley boys adore the Reverend Sewell.
And now I've come to spend some anxious hours
Prostrate before her threshold, crowned with flowers.
Such was the custom, as good scholars know,
Of classic lovers long long time ago.
And if they doubt it, let them please to look
At my sixth line, ode twenty-fifth, first book ;
And as a penance let them learn by heart
The note by Anthon, and the verse by Smart.

                    Sings.

  "Wake, O wake, my soul's enchantress !
    Listen to your lover's pleadings.
    Recognise in each effusion
    Doctor Bentley's various readings.

course of instruction in clerical and public elocution : an undertaking in
which the undergraduates of the day chose to discover something
ludicrous.

Fair as golden Aphrodite ;
Piquante as Rebecca Sharpe ;
Worthy of the pen of Trollope ;
Theme for old Anacreon's harp ;
Colder than out-college breakfasts ;*
Harder than the Old Court stones ;
Beam upon me from the window ;
Have compassion on my groans."

[HORACE *lies down on the threshold of* LYDIA'S *house.*
LYDIA *opens the door, and stumbles over him.*

Lyd.—Plague take you, Horace ! See, you've torn my
    gown.
Get up—and don't stay sprawling like the clown
Who lies with fiendish craft athwart the floor,
Then knocks at some unconscious tradesman's door.
Come, don't look like a fool, because you're not one.
But use your tongue :—at least if you have got one.

    Hor. [*Getting up*].—When like Diana's orb, serene and
    bright,
You rise resplendent on my aching sight,
My senses with a strange emotion swim,
And a cold shudder runs through every limb.
My eyes are dazzled, and my features glow,
As when a student in the Little-Go
Draws from his breast a surreptitious Paley,
Notes the contents, and floors the paper gaily ;
Then sees with horror in the gallery frowning
Some dread examiner from Cat's or Downing.

---

* The kitchen being within the Great Court, it is needless to describe the condition in which stewed kidneys or curried fish arrive at
lodgings distant some half mile from the college gate.

Lyd.—What have you brought me, Horace? You shall rue
 Unless it's something elegant and new.
  Hor.—Alas, my charmer, I have nought to bring.
I am too poor to buy a brooch or ring.
  Lyd.—Don't talk of brooches or of rings, you dove you,
'Tis for yourself, yourself alone, I love you.
Since I've been here I've had a hundred danglers,
Lords, fellow-commoners, and senior-wranglers,
Scholars, Smith's prizemen, deans, professors, dons,
Fellows of Trinity, and Queens', and John's ;
But none like you, from all that brilliant throng,
I've loved so readily, or loved so long.
Your wit's so racy, and your words so glowing,
Your dress so spicy, and your wink so knowing ;
Your songs are better than ten thousand purses.
So run me off some amatory verses.
I'll be your critic :—and beware, I tell ye,
You'll find me worse than Hermann or Orelli.
But first we'll try one figure of the dance,
A thought pronounced, that Balbus learned in France,
(Confound my stupid head! I mean in Gaul)
The year he brought me back my Cachmere shawl.
                              [*Dance. Exit* HORACE.
  Dec. M.—You faithless baggage, am I so much dirt,
That thus before my very nose you flirt?
Have I not lain whole evenings at your door?
My whole allowance spent, and hundreds more?
Did I not bet my money on a screw
That I might lose four dozen gloves to you,
White kid and primrose, sixes and a quarter?
Was it for this I jilted Gnatho's daughter?

Was it for this I got on the committee,*
And sent you all my tickets?   More's the pity!
  Lyd.—And if you did, though even that is false,
Did I not dance with you the fifteenth valse?
And would have tried a galoppe with you gladly,
Except for very shame, you waltzed so badly.
You purchased me the gloves, (may harpies tear them!)
But what of that? I let you see me wear them.
Do what you will: your time and money waste:
But pray allow me to consult my taste.
  Dec. M.—For your sake, Lydia, while you still were
        mine,
They gated me for half the term at nine:
And for your sake uncounted sums I owe
To Gent and Matthew, Litchfield, Ingrey, Rowe.
And yet you still my hand and heart despise,
Won by the glances of a freshman's eyes.
You and your minion all your lives shall cuss
The day you played the fool with Decius Mus.

                                    [*Exeunt.*

---

* The Committee of management of the Bachelors' Ball.

SCENE II.

The Rooms of HORACE.

BALBUS, CAIUS, HORACE, *and others, at table.*

SONG.

" Natis in usum lætitiæ."—ODE XXVII.   Book I.

To fight o'er cups for joy ordained
Suits well barbarian morals.
Let us our blushing Bacchus keep
From taint of bloody quarrels.

For Median daggers don't agree
With beer-cup rich and brown :
So rest your elbow on the couch,
And take your liquor down.

Come, drink about ! and, if you wish
That I should do the same,
I must request yon junior soph
To tell his sweetheart's name.

Bend close this way—Ah, wretched boy,
You're not her only suitor.
That lady has been long engaged
To our Assistant Tutor.

Dec. M.—Horace, your supper has been quite the thing.
You entertain as bravely as you sing.

I'm just three-quarters drunk, and tightly filled
With roast, and boiled, and stewed, and pulled, and grilled.
But there is one sad void within your doors,
One vacuum which nature most abhors.
For nought avails the spiced and bubbling bowl,
The pea in season, and the roe of sole,
Without fair woman, nature's proudest boast,
To pour the coffee and dispense the toast.

    Hor.—That shall be remedied, or Pluto's in it,
For I'm expecting Lydia every minute.

    Dec. M.—Things must be wonderfully changed of late
If she's allowed to pass the college gate.
I'll lay a mina on it.

    Hor.—   Done with you—
That she'll be here to-night.

    Dec. M.—   I'll make it two.

      Enter LYDIA *disguised as a Bedmaker.*

Sings—

    I make the butter fly, all in an hour :
        I put aside the preserves and cold meats,
  Telling my master his cream has turned sour,
      Hiding his pickles, purloining his sweets.
  I never languish for husband or dower :
      I never sigh to see gyps at my feet :
  I make the butter fly, all in an hour,
      Taking it home for my Saturday treat.
                [*Discovers herself.*

  Hor.   Well : Lydia dear, now you are here
        We'll have a game of loo, love ;
      Although I'm told the punch is cold
        With waiting long for you, love.

Lyd.   O, bother punch ! I've had my lunch,
           And afterwards some tea, love.
           A glass of sling is just the thing,
           And quite enough for me, love.

Enter SEMPRONIUS VIRIDIS, *a Freshman from Gallia Cisalpina.*

Hor.—Behold the prototype of Verdant Green !

S. V.—Are these the chambers of the Junior Dean ?

Hor.—Sir, I'm the Junior Dean.

S. V.—   I wish to state
The reason of my coming rather late
To early lecture on last Friday week.

Hor.—Young man, I bid you pause before you speak.
So grave a breach of college rules, by Castor,
Must come before no other than the Master.
In suppliant garb arrayed you'll duly call
Where stands his Lodge adjacent to the Hall.
There ask his pardon.   If he chance to scold,
Back your entreaties with a piece of gold.

                              [SEMPRONIUS *begins to go.*
Stay for a moment ; let me ask your name.

S. V.—Sempronius Viridis.

Hor.—   The very same !
I knew your father.   Tell me, if you can,
Does he not look an oldish sort of man ?

S. V.—Yes, that he does.

Hor.—   I fancied I was right.
Hair grey, or now perhaps a little white ?
Sit down, and join our company, my boy,
Let's give an hour to chat and social joy.
The gravest of us now and then unbends,
And likes his glass of claret and his friends.

Caius.—But first, my dear Sempronius, pray let us
Inquire if you've ascended Mount Hymettus
To see the term divide—for, if I'm right,
That incident comes off this very night.

    S. V.—Does it indeed! I thank you from my heart.
If that's the case it's almost time to start.
I don't like walking late in cap and gown,
For fear of being beaten by the town.

       [CAIUS *removes his gown, and substitutes his own,*
        which is old and ragged. Dance expressive of re-
        monstrance on the part of SEMPRONIUS, *and con-*
        tempt on that of the others. They hustle him out.

    Enter BRUTUS *and* CASSIUS *with Recruiting Ribbons.*

    Hor.—Why here's two heroes coming to recruit us.
What is your business, pray?

    Bru.—   I'm Marcus Brutus :
And this is Caius Cassius, a name,
Thanks to Will Shakspere, not unknown to fame.
We found our country groaning, and to ease her
We sent to his account great Julius Cæsar.
But young Augustus with a hungry pack
Of veteran troops came yelping on my track ;
While Antony, more truculent by far,
Cries " Havock !" and lets slip the dogs of war.
There must be here some smart young fellows willing
To serve their country, and to take the shilling.
We stand the uniform.

    Hor.—   And what's the pay?

    Bru.—Your beer, and twenty sesterces a day.
Coffee you'll get, as green as any leaf,
Fat pork, hard biscuits, and nice fresh boiled beef.

The bounty will be paid as best it can,
For Brutus is an honourable man.
Then there's the glory, and the smiles of beauty,
And some one else to take your turn of duty.
Is there one true-born son of Rome who fears
To meet the shock of Cæsar's hireling spears,
With me to conquer, or with me to die?
If any, speak! I pause for a reply.
    All.—None, Brutus, none.
    Bru.—   Then none have I offended.
But now we'll go! 'Tis time this scene were ended.
We start to-morrow, by Apollo's grace,
On the main route for Macedon and Thrace.
So get your kits packed up, and don't be late.
The convoy's due at seven fifty-eight.

                             [Exeunt omnes.

SCENE III.

The Senate-House. AUGUSTUS, MÆCENAS, *the* VICE-CHAN-
CELLOR, *the* PUBLIC ORATOR, DECIUS MUS, LYDIA,
STUDENTS *in the Gallery, etc.*

    V. C.—Your Royal Highness, wearied with the jars
Of civil discord and intestine wars,
Has for a while withdrawn you from the strife
To taste the sweets of Academic life:
And we have done our utmost to prepare
A varied and enticing bill of fare.

First, with absorbing interest you'll see
Mæcenas take an honorary degree.
Next, Decius Mus—of whom we're justly proud,
A youth with parts and modesty endowed,
On whom our fondest expectations hang—
Will speak a complimentary harangue :
Which will be followed by a feast in hall,
Succeeded by a supper and a ball.

 Aug.—Think you that to a fool I've such affinity
As to consent to dine in hall in Trinity?
I thank you for the kindness that you show ;
And in return this favour I bestow.
In honour of my uncle I will found
A Julian scholarship, worth sixty pound.
Examiners,—the lecturer on Greek,
The preacher at St. Mary's for the week,
The last Seatonian prizeman, and the Deans
Of Pembroke, Corpus, Sidney, Christ's, and Queens'.
They will examine, such are my intentions,
In plane astrology of three dimensions. [*Applause.*
And in return, for purposes of state,
I shall make bold to take the college plate,
And lay a tax of ninety-nine per cent
On all the fellows' stipends and the rent.
          [*Great sensation.*
And now we will proceed, if so you please,
At once to the conferring of degrees.

   PUBLIC ORATOR *leads up* MÆCENAS.

Pub. Or.—Præsento tibi hunc baccalaureum, cui reserva-
tur sua senioritas.   [*Cheering.*
 V. C.—Mæcenas, vir amplissime, edite atavis regibus.

               E

O et præsidium et dulce decus nostrum, confirmo tibi tuam
senioritatem.　Neque dubitari potest, vir reverende atque
doctissime, quin si natum haberem tuo ingenio præditum,
omnes omnia bona dicerent, et laudarent fortunas meas—

STUDENTS *in the Gallery.*
Three cheers for Caius Cæsar!
Three groans for Mr. Bright!
And now, in hopes to please her,
Three cheers for the lady in white!
Hurrah for the 'Varsity boat!
Hurrah for Robinson's vote!*

V.C.—Since classic phrases pall on minds so weak,
'Tis time for Decius Mus to rise and speak!
Dec. M.—Let me unfold before your royal ear
The doings of the Academic year.
Religious education and sound knowledge
Have flourished generally throughout the college:
Although the chapel-clerks, astounding fact,
For every surplice seven-and-six exact.
The porters too, who really should know better,
Charge us a halfpenny for every letter.†

* The mastership of St. Catharine's Hall fell vacant in 1861.
The electors with whom the appointment lay were five in number, of
whom two were candidates—Mr. Robinson and Mr. Jameson.　Of the
other three votes Mr. Jameson got two, and Mr. Robinson one.　Mr.
Jameson voted for Mr. Robinson, and Mr. Robinson for himself, thus
securing the mastership.　Through the cloud of pamphleteering and
pasquinading which has been floating about intermittently ever since
one fact is discernible:—that Mr. Robinson continued to hold the
mastership after he had become aware that Mr. Jameson was dissatisfied
with the transaction.

　† This impost dated from the time when the postage of letters was
heavy, and demanded a plentiful store of cash and careful accounts on
the part of the officer whose business it was to take in the correspondence

The fellowships have gone, save one in three,
In inverse ratio to the degree :
And we expect next year a junior op
Will, by the aid of bookwork, come out top.*
We've a hall steward, who becomes the place,
And draws his salary with wondrous grace :
But no one can perceive, as I 'm a sinner,
A very marked improvement in the dinner.
We still consume, with mingled shame and grief,
Veal that is tottering on the verge of beef ;
Veal void of stuffing, widowed of its ham,
Or the roast shoulder of an ancient ram.
Illustrious founder of a mighty line,
Go forth, and seize the sceptre that is thine !
Thou who hast studied in thine uncle's school :
For he did rear a race he might not rule,
(Although he paid for it uncommon dear) :
So thou shalt rule a race thou didst not rear.† [*Applause.*

of a numerous body of people, most of whom could read and write with
ease. Those who have the principal interest in the question,—the
porters themselves,—credit the couplet with the abolition of the tax.

* In the first edition the above four lines, the dearest the writer ever
penned, were suppressed at the last moment, and fresh matter sub-
stituted. But a thrifty bookbinder used the rejected pages to strengthen
the covers of a certain number of copies : so that the reader could
gratify his curiosity by the simple process of holding up the binding to
the light. Few could be induced to believe that the author was not a
party to this suicidal policy.

† These lines were a parody on a passage well known at the time,
occurring in the prize poem on the subject of "The Prince of Wales at
the tomb of Washington."

   For he did rear a race he might not rule.
   So thou shalt rule a race thou didst not rear.

The university lyre, which for long past had given forth very feeble
strains, was just then falling into the hands of a Cheltenham freshman,
who in this performance gave promise that has been worthily fulfilled in
the very little which he has hitherto given to the world.

Aug.—Upon my word, young man, you make me proud,
Although you need not bellow quite so loud.
So well you've learnt your speech, so nicely said it,
It does yourself and your instructors credit.
And therefore, in return, I'll not refuse
Whatever boon you ask.   Look sharp and choose.

Dec. M.—Then will your highness get me back, I pray,
A female slave of mine who's run away?
There stands the wench, blue-girdled round the waist.

Aug.—By Hercules, this Decius Mus has taste.
Well, since you say she's yours in justice, take her;
And if she won't go with you—why, I'll make her.

Lyd.—Sir, I entreat you by her name that bore you,
By that dear maid whose beaming eyes adore you.
Save me, O save me, from that bitter fate,
To be betrayed to one I scorn and hate.
I hate him, for he's rude, untidy, black,
In debt to Parfitt, Warwicker, and Flack.
To sum up all, deny it if he can,
A jealous, hideous, odious ten-year man.

Aug.—Take off the girl !

Lyd.   Oh, Sire !

Aug.   Have done, I say !
I can't be waiting here the livelong day.

[LYDIA *is dragged off.   Scene changes.*

SCENE IV.

In front of Brutus's *Tent.*

Horace *on guard.* *Enter* Caius.

Cai.—Horace, my boy, I thought I heard you singing,
And so I've come, these slight refreshments bringing.
We'll drain a bumper to your absent Lydia,
The sweetest girl from Britain to Pisidia.
And that reminds me.   Some one in the band
Has brought a letter, in a female hand,
Addressed to you : an obol to be paid.
                         [Caius *delivers the letter.*
Hor.—There's something wrong with Lydia, I'm afraid.
What's this? [*Reads.*] " My Horace, 'tis not yet too late
" To save your darling from a dreadful fate.
" The fatal time draws nigh.   Haste, haste, and save !"
                         [*Dashes down the letter.*
Shall Lydia be my faithless rival's slave ?
Caius, 'tis now the time to come down handsome :
You shall provide the money for her ransom.
    Cai.—But all my ready cash has gone in liquor
For your consumption.
    Hor.   Well then, pawn your ticker.
    Cai.—But why not pawn your own ?
    Hor.   Oh, heartless friend,
Your selfish words my tender bosom rend.

Was it for this I loved you as myself?
Was it for this I freely shared your pelf?
Was it for this your board I nightly graced,
And criticized your wines with faultless taste?

Sings.

We were fresh together.
I never can forget
How in October weather
On Parker's Piece we met;
Nor how in hall we paid so dear
For shapeless lumps of flesh,
And sized for cheese and college beer,
When you and I were fresh.

We were Junior Sophs together,
And used one Paley card.*
They plucked my every feather,
A usual fate, but hard.
You got the Craven and the Bell,
While I in folly's mesh
Without a single struggle fell,
When you and I were fresh.

---

* The card alluded to was an epitome of The Evidences of Christ-
ianity, which work formed one among the subjects of the Little-go ex-
amination. In this synopsis doctrinal arguments were summed up in
rude Hexameters and Pentameters for the assistance of treacherous
memories. The eleven proofs of the authenticity of the Historical
Scriptures were contained in the lines :
    Quoted, sui generis, vols, titles, publicly, comment,
    Both sides, without doubt, attacked, catalogue, apocryphal.
The learning by heart of this barbarous jargon was an important element
in that religious training, on the pretext of preserving which inviolate the
yearly bills for admitting nonconformists to the privileges and emolu-
ments of our universities have been talked out of the Commons or
kicked out of the Lords.

We're Questionists together ;
    We both have reached the verge
And limit of our tether,
    The hood of fur and serge.
Though this should be a Federal firm,
    And that a hot Secesh,
We'd fondly still recall the term
    When you and I were fresh.

Enter BRUTUS, *at the head of his army.*

Bru.—Halt ! Right face ! 'tention ! Don't be crowd-
    ing there !
You seem to think we're forming hollow square.
Now, since this neighbourhood is somewhat damp,
To-morrow morning we shall strike our camp,
And, having marched some twenty miles with unction,
Take up our ground beyond Philippi junction.
When the first beams of Sol the meadows kiss
Be all of you prepared to start. Dis-miss !
                    [*Exeunt all but* BRUTUS.

The Stage grows dark.

There's nothing stirring all along the line.
Boy, place a chair, and bring a flask of wine.
I'll sit awhile alone, and drown my sorrow,
And think about my tactics for to-morrow.
       [*Sits and sips. Ghost of* CÆSAR *rises, to music.*
Unless I'm wrong, this Massic's rather fruity.
I'll have another bottle.
   Ghost.   Et tu, Brute !

SONG AND DANCE.

I shrink from the light,
But at dead of night
In a ghastly polka skip I :
And all this way
I've come to say
That I'll meet you again at Philippi.

Bru.   I very much rue .
That I ran you through,
I've been a terrible rip, I :
But please, Sir, don't,
I hope you won't
Ever meet me again at Philippi.

.

Ghost.   By the light of the moon
I have come full soon
All armed with Tisiphone's whip, I :
Your sins shall be lashed,
And your hopes all dashed,
When I meet you again at Philippi.

[*Exeunt dancing.*

SCENE V.

The Plains of Philippi. BRUTUS *and* CASSIUS, *at the head of their army.*

Bru.—Cassius, the fatal hour is drawing nigh.
The time has come to conquer or to die.
That veteran force at which you daily scoff
Is marching to the fight some furlongs off :

While all our three-months' volunteers go home,
And meet a cordial welcome back to Rome.
'Tis time to form my soldiers for the fight.
Fall in ! Attention ! Number from the right !
> [*That manœuvre takes place with the usual success.
> The Army marches out. Alarms. Excursions.
> The Army rushes in again in confusion.*

Enter QUINTUS RUSSELLUS MAXIMUS.

Rus.—What means this most discreditable bustle ?
I am the correspondent, Quintus Russell.
Describe the enemy, that I may draw him.
   Sol.—We can't describe him, for we never saw him.
   Rus.—You never saw the foe ! This is indeed
A most confused, unsoldierlike stampede.
I never met with such a shameful scene,
As daily correspondent though I've been
(At least I doubt if you will find a dailyer)
In every fight from Munda to Pharsalia.
My military knowledge is not small.
I witnessed Cæsar's first campaign in Gaul,
And found myself in an unpleasant mess
For making known his tactics through the press.
The late reforms, as e'en the Horse-guards own,
Are due to me, and due to me alone.
Give me the standard ! On to martial deeds !
None dare turn craven when their critic leads !
This foul dishonour from your annals wipe !
Whoever runs shall read his name in type.
   Sol.—Now by our free and most enlightened nation
We'll teach this Britisher to know his station.

We are afraid of being killed, 'tis true :
But strike me blind if we're afraid of you !
We'll tar and feather you from head to tail,
And ride you round the country on a rail.
Scene-painter, lend us all your brushes, pray.
We'll take our chance of what the *Times* may say.

> [*They seize* QUINTUS RUSSELLUS MAXIMUS.

Enter CASSIUS *and* BRUTUS.

Rus.—Release me, Brutus !   In the English press
I'll say you gained a glorious success.
I will indeed !   Or, if it suit you better,
You shall yourself compose to-morrow's letter.
Stain not your spotless name with useless crimes !
O save the correspondent of the *Times!*

Bru.—Forbear, my soldiers !   For 'tis most absurd
To make a correspondent like a bird.
Protect the baggage, lest their stragglers loot us.

> [*Exeunt* SOLDIERS.

Fly, stranger, fly, and bless the name of Brutus !

> [*Exit* QUINTUS RUSSELLUS MAXIMUS.

All hope has faded.   Cassius, be not weak.
Fate closes in.   Together must we seek
That undiscovered country from whose bourn
No uncommercial travellers return.
Present thy sword, and when I give the sign
Fall on my point, and I will fall on thine.

Cas.—Ah, Brutus, this fond faithful heart will burst.
I love you far too well to die the first :
But when I've mourned thy death with many a groan
I'll bid thy life-blood mingle with mine own.

Bru.—Well, be it so.   Hold out the fatal blade.
One ! two ! three !   Off !   Confound it, who's afraid ?
      [*Rushes on the sword, and falls.*
This was the way I died, but they relate, O,
That I was murdered by my freedman Strato.
     [*Dies.   Cassius takes his purse, and runs*
      off with an air of relief.

    Enter HORACE *humming.*

Hor.—The minstrel-boy from the wars is gone,
   All out of breath you'll find him ;
  He has run some five miles off and on,
   And his shield has flung behind him.
I hope this spot is out of range of fire.
Why ! here's the general prostrate in the mire,
Dead as a stoker on the Brighton line !
Speak, my lord Brutus !   Speak !   He gives no sign.
Woe worth the day !   Woe worth this fatal field !
I've lost my leader, thrown away my shield.
My mother charged me, as she tied her bonnet,
To come back either with it or upon it.
My honour could endure no worse disaster
Unless I'd voted for myself as Master.
I'm sure I heartily repent, by Juno,
Quod mihi pareret legio Romana tribuno.   [*Exit.*

SCENE VI.

The head-quarters of AUGUSTUS, *near Philippi.*

AUGUSTUS, MÆCENAS, DECIUS MUS, LYDIA, HORACE *in custody*, SOLDIERS, GUARDS, ETC.

Soldier.—My Lord, while foraging the country round,
Our skirmishers this prisoner have found ;
Who, by his gallant mien and splendid coat,
We guess will prove an officer of note.
He ran so quickly from the scene of strife
That his must be a valuable life.
    Aug.—So young, and yet a rebel !   Oh, for shame !
Are any here acquainted with his name?
    Dec. M.—This wretched youth, a nursling of sedition,
At Athens College holds an exhibition,
Which would have gone to me, without a doubt,
Had but the founder's will been carried out.
When Rome your highness for her consul chose
He ventured at the Union to propose
" That this assembly views with reprobation
" A measure fraught with danger to the nation."
A motion which, although opposed by me,
Was passed by eighty votes to twenty-three.
And in his ode, conceive it if you can, Sir,
He dared insert a most Horatian stanza
Which speaks of Tully as our forum's pride,
A man he knows your highness can't abide.
    Aug.—Enough, his guilt is proved, at least to me.
Rig up a gallows on the nearest tree !

What, in reply to all we just have heard,
Can you allege that sentence be deferred?

Hor.—My loved protector, patron kind and true
Of hapless genius, I appeal to you,
To you, Mæcenas, sprung from royal stock,
My sweetest glory, and my guardian rock.
There are whom it delights with wondrous gust
To have collected the Olympic dust—

Mæc.—Perhaps so, but I can't discover quite
How that will help you in your present plight.
Unless your circumstances greatly alter
You're much more likely to collect a halter.
Augustus, spare this most unlucky lad
Who's far too idle to be very bad.
He sings a sparkling song, can write a bit,
And boasts some talent, impudence, and wit.
He's asked to every supper in the town;
He got a Camden, and he halved a Browne;*
And, as a coping-stone to all his praise,
He took a seventh class in both his Mays.

Aug.—Well, if this budding hero is a poet,
We soon will find some means to make him show it.
To 'scape the consequences of your frolic
Be pleased to parody the tenth Bucolic.

Hor.—What haunts detain you on this ill-starred day,
      Castalian Muses, say?†

---

* Of late years the Browne medal for Latin and Greek epigrams
had been divided between the successful competitors in the respective
languages: to the annual disgust of both the half-medallists; each of
whom, with the partiality of an author, regarded himself as having lost
by the change of system.

   †   "Quæ nemora aut qui vos saltus habuere, puellæ
     Naiades," &c.

What seat of classic lore, what hallowed stream?
         Strayed you by sedgy Cam,
         While from the Barnwell dam
You watch the gambols of the silver bream?
         Or by the willows weeping
         O'er Cherwell slowly creeping
Swoll'n with the suds of many an ancient hall
Past Jowett's cloistered cell and Stanley's stall?
Or have ye flown, invoked in boyish song,
         To Harrow's far-seen hill?
         Or hard by Avon's rill
Beloved of Hughes the earnest and the strong,
And along Barby-road, and round the Island Goal,
And Caldecott's famed spinney do ye stroll
         On this unhappy morn
When fair Venusia's tuneful swain
Trembling all in captive chain
With drooping eyes endures the victor's scorn?—

Aug.—Well done!   You really have a turn for rhyme.
I think we'll hear the rest another time.
Mæcenas, you'll impress on him, I hope,
How very narrowly he missed the rope.
I'll give your protegé, still more to pleasure ye,
A nomination in the public Treasury.
So be prepared to pass, on this day week,
In hydrostatics, German, French, and Greek,
One eastern language, botany, precis,
(I don't exactly know what that may be,
Nor do I long to probe the fearful mystery,)
Pure mathematics, law, and modern history.

And as for Decius Mus,—well, stop a bit,
I think I know a post for which he's fit,
(Unless indeed our partial feelings warp us ;)—
I'll make him English lecturer at Corpus.
There let him work a total revolution
In Clerical and Public Elocution.

    Hor.—My lord Augustus, by the Gods above,
This one prayer grant me! Give me back my love.
Without my Lydia life itself is loss,
And Treasury clerkships seem but so much dross.
Restore my darling! Well your poet knows
To pay what debt of gratitude he owes.

    Aug.—Let mistress Lydia pick, and pray make haste,
Whiche'er of these two fellows suits her taste.
Our judgment shall be guided by her voice.
I cannot say I envy her the choice.

        "Donec gratus eram tibi."—ODE IX. BOOK III.

Hor.   While still you loved your Horace best
        Of all my peers who round you pressed,
        (Though not in expurgated versions)
        More proud I lived than King of Persians.

Lyd.   And while as yet no other dame
        Had kindled in your breast a flame,
        (Though Niebuhr her existence doubt)
        I cut historic Ilia out.

Hor.   Dark Chlöe now my homage owns,
        With studied airs, and dulcet tones ;
        For whom I should not fear to die,
        If death would pass my charmer by.

Lyd. I now am lodging at the rus-
In-urbe of young Decius Mus.
Twice over would I gladly die
To see him hit in either eye.

Hor. But should the old love come again,
And Lydia her sway retain?
If to my heart once more I take her,
And bid dark Chlöe wed the baker?

Lyd. Though you be treacherous as audit*
When at the fire you've lately thawed it,
For Decius Mus no more I'd care
Than for their plate the Dons of Clare.†

Aug.—In that case, whether you prefer or not,
I must insist you take her on the spot.
I'll give you, won by her transcendent charms,
The choicest of your patron's Sabine farms.
There shall you live 'midst garlands, wine, and rhymes,
The·darling of your own and future times;
And be translated, as a poet should,
In prose by Watson and in verse by Good.

---

* Connoisseurs treat audit ale like claret, and place it for a while in front of the fire: but the effect is seldom ascertained; for the corks, (such corks, at any rate, as fall to the portion of gentlemen in statu pupillari,) almost invariably leap from the bottles, and are followed by the best part of the ale.

† About this period the authorities of Clare College took it into their heads to sell at the price of old silver some fine plate, said to have been presented to their predecessors immediately after the restoration in order to replace that which had been sacrificed in darker times to the royal cause. The proceeding excited in virtuoso circles a good deal of contemptuous astonishment.

HORACE *and* LYDIA *embrace.*

Hor.   O the heavenly bliss
          Of that first long kiss,
     As in my arms I locked her ;
          When none need shout,
          "You fool, look out,
     "Here comes the Senior Proctor !"

Aug.   Light Hymen's torch,
          And deck the porch !
     May smiling Venus bless you !
          May Chian flow,
          And roses blow,
     And critics ne'er distress you !

Hor.   But now 'tis late,
          The college gate
     Has long been shut, I 'm certain.
          So thus, kind friends,
          Our story ends,
     And we must drop the curtain.

F

THE CAMBRIDGE DIONYSIA:

A CLASSIC DREAM.

THE CAMBRIDGE DIONYSIA:

A CLASSIC DREAM.

IN the year 1858 there appeared at Cambridge the "Lion," a magazine very creditably conducted, written chiefly or entirely by undergraduates. It displayed Transcendental tendencies, which, combined with the belief that some of the contributors knew a good deal of German and the certainty that others knew very little Latin, excited the bitter wrath of those young men who aspired to classical honours, and among them of the author, who parodied the first number in a performance entitled the "Bear." A second number of the obnoxious publication soon followed, and produced the "Cambridge Dionysia," which was written in a frenzy of boyish indignation. The "Lion" survived this renewed assault, and got eventually into a third number :—which for a University periodical may be considered an instance of longevity.

The prose portion of the "Dionysia" was written for a circle of readers who were obliged from the necessities

of their position annually to make themselves masters of
the smallest details in the celebration of the Bacchic
festivals; and may still amuse such of them as retain their
hold on the main outlines of that somewhat unprofitable
field of knowledge.   The verse is in imitation of an
Athenian Comedy.   Whether it be that the author's mind
was at the time more Greek than English :—or that Cambridge society was so limited as to admit of the personal
allusions being generally intelligible, and, if truth be told,
rather scurrilous:—or that the style and tone of a writer
are most readily assimilated by those at his own period
of life; (and, according to the received chronology, the
great poet produced the Knights and the Acharnians while
emerging from his teens :)—from some or all of these
causes it happens that this trifle, while most inadequately
representing the humour, the vigour, the fertility, the
exquisite fancy of the comedian, faithfully enough repro-
duces his mannerism.   Among the more superficial Aristophanic qualities which the "Dionysia" reflects may be
included a wilful ignorance of the subjects satirised.   The
author was at least as hopelessly unacquainted with the
notions of Emerson as Aristophanes was with the tenets
of Socrates : whose teaching he supposed to consist in
natural history, for which the philosopher had a strong

distaste, and in forensic rhetoric, for which he entertained an intense and immortal aversion.

The plot, and much of the text, are in pretty close paraphrase of the "Wasps" :—a drama widely known in the modern and rather awkward dress of Racine's "Plaideurs." By a fortunate chance the names of the two principal characters in the original play required nothing but the insertion of a single letter to adapt them for Cambridge use : and Philoleon answers to the Athenian dotard who is placed under tutelage by his own son, with feelings embittered by the reflection that he is "an only father." Happy time, when an undergraduate in his last year of residence seemed an impersonation of old age !

TRINITY COLLEGE, *November* 1858.

ON the first Audit-day of this year Shillibere, with whom I was engaged upon the Wasps of Aristophanes, told me that as it was the πιθοιγία* he would excuse my reading with him, but bade me get up the subject of the Dionysiac festivals against our next meeting. I took a longer walk than was my wont, and by hall-time was quite ready to appreciate the fact of its being a Feast. After dinner Barlow, the Bachelor Scholar, came to my rooms, and we sat late, drinking sherry, and discussing the merits of the ale at the different colleges. When he had gone I took down the Wasps, but somehow or other I could not make much of them. So I drew my easy-chair to the fire, filled my pipe, and opened Smith's Antiquities on the article "Dionysia." But the Greek words bothered me, and I was too lazy to rise for a Lexicon. So I fell a thinking on Athens, and what glorious fun the festival must have been. I can recollect nothing more till I found myself in the midst of a strange dream. And yet, marvellous as it was, nothing seemed to surprise me; but I took it for granted that everything was perfectly natural and consistent. And the dream was as follows :

I was still sitting in my rooms with my books before me : but it was broad daylight, and a lovely morning, such

---

* The classic mind of the great coach might well find an analogy between the day in the rubric of old Athens which derived its name from the opening of the casks to taste the wine of the preceding year, and the day in the calendar of modern Trinity when by solemn custom the fresh brew of college ale flows in mediæval abundance.

as sometimes breaks upon us, even at Cambridge, in the beginning of November. The courts were very quiet, but I heard a constant shouting in the distance, as if there was some tumult in the streets. Suddenly the door flung open, and Barlow appeared. He looked flushed and excited; on his head was a garland of ivy-leaves, and he swung in his hand a pewter. "Shut up your books," he cried: "no reading on the πιθοιγία. If you do another equation I'll inform against you for impiety. The God, the jolly God, hates Colenso worse than he hated Pentheus. I've come to fetch you to the theatre, whether you will or no. There is a new comedy to be represented, and all the University will be there. By Hercules, I hope they'll hit the authorities hard. When the performance is over we sup with Rumbold of Caius, culinary Caius, the head-quarters of good living. I am king of the feast, and not a soul shall get off under three bottles. We have stolen the chaplets from the Botanical Gardens; Ingrey sends the dessert, and Stratton has promised to bring two flute-players from Barn——." Here I started up, crying, " Barlow, lead on ! I'm your man." And we danced out of the New Court gate, and up the lane into Trinity-street. And there was a sight that made my heart leap.

The whole road was crowded with men, all in the wildest state of joy and liquor. Every one acknowledged the presence of the God, to whom liberty and license are dear. Laughing, singing, cheering, jesting, they were pouring in an unbroken stream towards Magdalen-bridge. Gyps mingled with the throng, enjoying perfect freedom and equality on this day of the year. Ever and anon some fresh band of revellers issued from the colleges and lodging-houses on the way, and swelled the main flood. Here came a mob of Queens' men, sweeping the street, and roaring at the pitch of their voices, "For he's a jolly good fellow:" referring probably to the late senior wrangler. There, from the great gate of Harry the Eighth, streamed forth the whole club of Third Trinity. In front, arm-in-arm, strode the victorious four; while elevated on the shoulders of the crew of the second boat sat the secretary, his temples crowned with roses, riding a huge barrel, and bearing in his hand a silver bowl foaming with cider-cup. As we passed All Saints'-passage, from the direction of the Hoop Inn there moved a goodly company, twenty-five or thirty in number, and my companion whispered me that this was the Historical Society, and bawled out to them to ask whether Elizabeth was justified in putting Mary to death.* And just inside the gateway of St. John's College there was a group of young men who successively tried to dance on an inflated pigskin. And he who danced best received a draught of their ale. And presently there came by a drunken Trinity sizar, who, after a successful trial, took the flagon, but when he had tasted, he cursed, and spit, and swore no Trinity shoe-black would condescend to drink it. Upon which a stout Johnian kicked his shins, and, as it was evident that trouble would ensue, and that we as men of the same College would be implicated in it, we hurried away, not wishing to desecrate the festival of the God by evil feelings. And on Magdalen-bridge was seated a knot of idle fellows who chaffed all the passers-by. And among others they

---

* The Historical Society took its rise at a time when the debates at the Union had given such an impulse to oratory that men were found who thought once a week not often enough for discussing to what extent Hampden was legally authorised in resisting the imposition of ship-money, and whether Addison or the Duke of Marlborough most deserved the admiration of posterity.

told a solitary individual in a Downing-gown that he was so few that his College did not think it worth its while to brew for him, but had sent out for a gallon of swipes from the Eagle for his special consumption. So at last we arrived at the gate of the theatre, and after paying three-pence each, which had been furnished us from the University Chest, we went in and sat down.

One side of the Castle-hill had been hollowed out into a spacious theatre. Tier above tier the long benches rose to the summit of the slope. In the front seats were the Vice-chancellor, and the heads of colleges, and doctors of divinity, and professors, and noblemen, and all who could claim founders' kin. And the rest of the space was filled to overflowing with undergraduates and bachelors. But all females were excluded from the spectacle. And the throng was very clamorous, and many were provided with oranges, and nuts, and even stones, wherewith to pelt the unpopular actors. And in the orchestra was an altar, at which Shillibere stood, crowned with ivy, and robed in a long white robe. And from time to time he poured copious libations of ale upon the ground.

And the stage was veiled with a great curtain, embroidered with the loves and deeds of ancient and godlike men. And there I saw how the chosen heroes had launched a boat of pristine build, and ventured down the river in search of the Golden Fleece, where, as rumour said, the beer which the immortals drank was brewed. And I saw too how, as they passed along the black water, the first prow which had ploughed those waves, the men of Barnwell came down to the shore to wonder at the strange sight. And how, near the Stygian ferry, they came upon a fierce race, who seized their boat with long poles, and threw with unerring aim brickbats which ten bargemen of these days would in vain attempt to lift. And how, when at length they had found the Golden Fleece, their young chief was captured by the landlord and his friends, and locked up in darkness and solitude. But the black-haired daughter of the inn, who was cunning at medicating ales and knew the virtues of strychnine and all bitter herbs, was charmed with the flowing ringlets and easy tongue of the youth. And she stole the key from her father while he was overcome with drink, and eloped to the boat with her new lover.

All this I saw, and much more. And next me sat a staid bachelor, who seemed as if he had taken no part in the jollity of the morning. So we fell into conversation, and he told me how the theatre had been built under the inspection of Dr. Donaldson, from a comparison of plans furnished by freshmen in the Trinity College examinations. And he said that the festival of this year was jovial beyond any that had preceded it; for that the public mind had just recovered from the painful excitement caused by the mutilation of the statues on the roof of Trinity library: which act men had suspected to be part of a plot for overturning the constitution of the University, and delivering us over to the Commissioners. And that report said there would be two Choruses in this play. And that fourteen First Trinity jerseys had been ordered from Searle's, and one of great size for the Coryphæus. And he would have said more, but a tipsy Pembroke man bade him hold his tongue, or he would bring against him an action of sacrilege at the next private business meeting in the Union, for disturbing the worship of the God. So we looked, and the curtain had already been drawn down. And the scene disclosed was in the Old Court of Trinity, letter Z; and two gyps were asleep

outside the door; and the clock struck six, and first one
started up, and then the other.

Gyp A.—I dreamed we both were waiting in the Hall
Serving refreshments at the Bachelors' Ball.
There, gayest trifler in the throng of dancers,
Was Clayton* cutting figures in the Lancers.
    Gyp B.—Well dreamt! But I have dreams as fine as
      you.
Here's one as marvellous, and just as true.
Methought I heard our Rhadamanthine Mayor
Deal justice from the magisterial chair.
A Corpus sizar had been well-nigh slain
By fifteen blackguards in St. Botolph's lane.
The Mayor approved his fellow-townsmen's pluck,
And fined the plaintiff two-pound-ten for luck.
As pensively he rubbed his broken head,
" Confound old Currier Balls !" the gownsman said.†
    Gyp A.—Come now, I'll chat a little with the audience.
Our master here, who keeps in the top-story,
Honest Philoleon, for his first three years
Led a most quiet and gentlemanly life.
He was not gated more than twice a term ;
He read three hours a-day; rode every week ;

---

* This gentleman preached an annual sermon against the Bachelors'
Ball: a festival about which reading men talked a great deal, but at
which they would as soon have thought of appearing as Mr. Clayton
himself.

  † In this autumn frequent collisions occurred between the boating-
men of the University and the police. The most obnoxious member
of the force was a certain 20 C, or 20 K, who is more than once alluded
to in the course of this Drama. Mr. Balls, the Mayor for the time
being, had pretty constantly to sit in judgment on cases of assault and
battery.

Last year pulled seven in our second boat.
In all things moderation was his motto.
But now he's gone stark mad; and you must guess
What sort his madness is.*   [*To the spectators.*

Gyp B.—That Queens' man there
Says that he's bent on being senior wrangler.†

Gyp A.—No, no; he won't be old enough these ten
years.

Gyp B.—And that black-whiskered noisy party yonder,
Sitting amongst a group of Harrow freshmen,‡
Guesses he aims at office in the Union.

Gyp A.—What, to be called united and compact,
And to be chaffed in the suggestion book?
Not quite so low as that.   Come, try again.
D'ye give it up?   Well, listen, and I'll tell you.
One Sunday evening last May term at tea
He met by chance a troop of roaring Lions,

---

*   ἐπεὶ τοπάζετε.
'Αμυνίας μὲν ὁ Προνάπου φήσ' οὑτοσὶ
εἶναι φιλόκυβον αὐτόν· κ.τ.λ.—Wasps, line 73.

† Queens' college carried off the blue riband in the years 1857 and 1858, in the person of champions who, according to the gossip of the senate-house, were by some years senior to their competitors.

‡ During the spring of 1858 a ministerial crisis occurred in the Union Society. The official element had become unpopular among the mass of the boating-men : whom in their turn the bureaucracy stigmatised by the epithet of "the bargees." The most noisy orator of the opposition was a Harrow freshman : who, upon one occasion, began a withering peroration with the words "there they sit, compact, united :" indicating at the same time the Government bench by a sweep of the arm : an amount of gesticulation so unprecedented within those walls as to convulse the audience with emotion. Party spirit at length ran so high, and the attendance was consequently so large, that a stand-and-fall division was taken in the neighbouring auction-rooms ; the Union itself having become nearly as uncomfortable as the House of Commons on an ordinary business night.

And came back swearing he must join their number,
Or give up hopes of immortality.
From that day forth he ran about the college,
Talking of " Truth," and " Realised Ideals";
And asking men to give him a $\pi o\hat{v}\ \sigma\tau\hat{\omega}$;*
And telling them he saw within their eyes
Symptoms which marked affinity of souls.
So, in this state of things, his younger brother
Bdelyleon came up this term to College,
A sensible sharp-tempered Eton freshman ;
Who, when he saw his brother's strange distemper,
Blushed for himself and for the family.
And first he tried by pleasing the old fellow
To wean him from his hobby ; taught him songs,
And took him out to supper : but whenever
His health was drunk, and he was asked to sing,
He spoke straight off a canto from " St. Clair."†
And then he dressed him in his best, and washed him,
And got him made a member of the Musical :
But, at the first rehearsal, off he ran,
His fiddle on his back, and never stopped
Till he was inside Palmer's Printing-office.
So, vexed and wearied at his constant folly,
The young one locked him up within his rooms,
And placed us here on sentry, day and night.
But the old chap is sly, and full of tricks,
And loves his liberty.

　　　　　　　[PHILOLEON *appears at the window.*

---

　　* " Give us a $\pi o\hat{v}\ \sigma\tau\hat{\omega}$, and we will move the world."—Extract
from the Preface to the " Lion."

　　† A poem in Octosyllabics, entitled " St. Clair," was among the
contributions to the " Lion", which was published by Mr. Palmer.

Phil.—Hallo, you scoundrel!
Just let me out : 'tis time to go to lecture.
  Gyp A.—Why you're a questionist : you have no lectures.
[*Enter* BDELYLEON.

  Bdel.—Was ever freshman plagued with such a brother?
What have I done that I deserve this evil?
I never was undutiful ; I never
Have read a line of Alexander Smith ;
Nor picked a pocket ; nor worn peg-top trousers ;
Nor taken notes at any college lecture.
Who calls dame Fortune blind does not bely her.
  Phil.—I want a supper order from my tutor.
  Bdel.—No, no, old boy, I took good care of that :
I got you an ægrotat. Sold again !
Where are you now? Good heavens !
[PHILOLEON *puts his head out of the chimney.*
  Phil.   I'm the smoke.*
  Bdel.—Confound the man who altered all our chimneys !
Jackson, run up, and beat him with the pewter
Till he backs water ; then clap on a sack.
[PHILOLEON *reappears at the window.*
  Phil.—O Lord St. Clair, on bended knee
I charge you set the maiden free !
  Bdel.—In mercy stop that nonsense quick.
Your Lion always makes me sick.
I feel as ill as when I tried
My first and only Smoker's Pride.
  Phil.—O may the curses of the Gods light on you !
And may you wallow in the lowest Hades,
Along with all the men who 've struck their Tutor,

----

* οὗτος, τίς εἶ σύ;
  καπνὸς ἔγωγ' ἐξέρχομαι.—*Wasps*, line 144.

Or laid against the boat-club of their College,
Or caught a crab just opposite the Plough :
In that sad place of punishment and woe
Where lectures last from early dawn till noon,
And where the gate-fines rival those at Christ's,
And there's a change of Proctors every week !*
Then you'll repent of having used me thus.

 Bdel.—You blasphemous old villain !   Come, you fellows,
We all must need some coffee this cold morning.

   [*Enter Chorus of writers of the " Lion," preceded*
    by a chorister bearing a lantern.

 Chorus A.—Rosy-fingered dawn is breaking o'er the
  fretted roof of King's.

Bright and frosty is the morning.   Sharp and clear each
  footfall rings.

Gyps across the court are hurrying with the early breads
  and butters.

Blithely hums the Master's butler while he's taking down
  the shutters.

In our rooms we left the kettle gaily singing on the coals ;

And within the grate are steaming eggs, and ham, and toast,
  and rolls.

Soon we'll have a jovial breakfast with the members of our
  mess,

Chatting of our darling project, future hopes, and past success.

We have come to fetch our brother.   What can cause his
  long delay?

It was not his wont to keep us shivering here the livelong day.

He was always sharp and sprightly when the Lion was in
  question ;

Ever ready with an Essay ; ever prompt with a suggestion.

  * New Proctors are as much dreaded in the quadrangles as new
ministers in the public offices.

Surely he must be offended
 At our leaving out his poem :
Yet no insult was intended,
 As our want of space must show him.
Or perchance he came home jolly,
 Wishing to knock down the porter,
And lies cursing at his folly
 With a tongue that tastes like mortar.
Shew yourself upon the landing :
 Hear your loved companions' groans :
For our feet are sore with standing
 On the rugged Old Court stones.

   [PHILOLEON *shews himself at the window.*

Phil.—Comrades, when I heard your voices, how my
 heart within me leapt !
Thoughts of happier days came o'er my spirit, and I almost
 wept :—
Those bright days when free and happy with some kindred
 soul I strayed
Talking of The Unconditioned up and down the chesnut
 glade.
Now a cruel younger brother keeps me under lock and key.
Those I hate are always by me. Those I love I may not
 see.
O my own, my cherished Lion, offspring of my cares and
 toil,
Would that I and thou were lying underneath the All Saints'
 soil !
Drop your voices, dear companions, lest you rouse a sleeping Bear.

 Chorus A.—Does he then despise our anger? All men
  know who ate Don't Care.

Never fear him! We'll protect you. Do not heed his
threats and frowns.

Say your prayers, and jump down boldly! We will catch
you in our gowns.

> [PHILOLEON *places his leg over the window-sill,*
> *but is seized from behind by* BDELYLEON.

Bdel.—Not so fast, you old deceiver! From your evil
courses turn.

Never will I tamely let you join in such a vile concern.

Sooner than behold my brother sunk to such a depth of scorn

Gladly would I bear to see him walking on a Sunday morn

'Twixt a pair of pupil-teachers, all the length of Jesus-lane,

With a school of dirty children slowly shambling in his train :

Or behold him in the Union, on the Presidential seat,

Shakspeare* smiling blandly o'er him, freshmen ranting at
his feet.

Get you gone, you pack of scoundrels! Don't stand bawling
here all day.

Williams, fetch me out the slop-pail : Jackson, run for 20 K !

Chorus A.—Slay the despot! Slay the tyrant! Him who
cannot brook to see

All his neighbours dwelling round him peaceable, secure,
and free.

Well I know you've long been plotting how to seize the
Castle-hill

With a band of hired assassins, there to work your cruel will.

Let the man who wrote "the Syrens" make a feint upon the
door :

Bring us ladders, ropes, and axes ; we must storm the second
floor.   [*Enter Chorus of First Trinity boating-men.*

---

* In the old Union a Shaksperian bust of more than ordinary
vapidity formed a prominent object above the head of the President.

Chorus B.—Here they are. Upon them boldly! Double
  quick across the grass!
Cut them off from Bishop's Hostel, lest along the wall they
  pass!
Forward, Darroch! Forward, Perring! Charge them, Lyle,
  and now remember
'Gainst what odds you fought and conquered on the fifth of
  last November:
When you broke with one brave comrade through an armed
  and murderous mob.
Fear not an æsthetic humbug, you who 've faced a Cambridge
  snob.
Men of twelve stone, in the centre! Coxswains, skirmish on
  the flank!
You 're too eager there, you youngsters: Jones and Prickard,
  keep your rank!
Do not stay to spoil the fallen while a soul is left alive:
We must smoke them out and kill them, now we 've caught
  them in the hive.

> [*They charge the writers in the " Lion,"*
> *who fly in all directions.*

Victory! Victory! now for a shout
As when we bumped the Johnians out!
Vain was the might of Elective Affinities
When brought face to face with our valiant First Trinities.
Victory! Victory! Huzza! Tantivy!
> For when a man
> Who can hardly scan
Talks of " the pictured page of Livy,"
'Tis time for every lad of sense
To arm in honesty's defence

As if the French were steaming over
In rams of iron from Brest to Dover.

> [Bdelyleon *comes out leading* Philoleon
> *dressed in a First Trinity costume.*

Bdel.—Thank you, my brave allies ! And now to prove
The confidence I have in your discretion
I here entrust to you my elder brother,
To watch his morals, and to cure his madness.
So treat him kindly ; put him in a tub,
And take him down the river every day ;
And see that no one asks him out to supper,
To make him tipsy. Be not hard upon him,
But let him have his pipe and glass of sherry,
Since he is old and foolish. And, if ever
He comes back sound in body and in mind,
I 'll stand you claret at the next club-meeting.

> [*Exit* Bdelyleon.

PARABASIS.

We wish to praise our poet, who despising fame and pelf
Flew like a bull-dog at the throat of the jagged toothed
　　monster itself*
Which rages over all the town, from Magdalene-bridge to
　　Downing,
With the bray of a dreamy German ass 'neath the hide of
　　Robert Browning.
But some of you good fellows think, as the poet grieves to
　　hear,
That you are laughed at in "the Bears," the play he wrote
　　last year :

　　θρασέως συστὰς εὐθὺς ἀπ' ἀρχῆς αὐτῷ τῷ καρχαρόδοντι.

> *Wasps,* line 1031.

So he assures you faithfully no insult was intended.
Do not cherish bitter feelings ; for least said is soonest
    mended.
        And next he bids us tax our wit
        To tell some members of the Pitt,
        Whose names he knows not, when they meet
        Him passing into Sidney-street,
        Not to bawl out " The Bear, The Bear !"
        First because he does not care :
        Then surely for a man of taste
        It is a sin and shame to waste
        In calling nicknames near the Hoop
        The breath that's given to cool our soup.
        So, being a good-tempered bard,
        Whichever of them leaves his card
        He'll ask him out next week to dine,
        And shake hands o'er a glass of wine.
And now he bids you all good evening, and farewell till
    next October ;
And hopes to-night you'll sup like princes, and that none
    will go home sober.
If policeman K arrests you, let not that your spirits damp :
Break his head, and shave his whiskers, and suspend him to
    the lamp.*

---

* This advice was taken only too literally. The officer in question, on the night of the First Trinity boat-supper, ventured within the gates of the college, and was there maltreated in a manner that led, if the author's recollection serves, to the incarceration of some of the offenders. The prosecutor commented with much severity upon the concluding lines of the " Dionysia."

THE DAWK BUNGALOW;

OR,

'IS HIS APPOINTMENT PUCKA?'

THE DAWK BUNGALOW;

OR, 'IS HIS APPOINTMENT PUCKA?'

THIS play takes its name from the comfortless hostelries of India: in which the larder consists of a live fowl, and the accommodation of three rooms on the ground-floor, less than half-furnished even according to Oriental notions of furniture: the traveller being supposed to bring with him bread, beer, and bedding. The leading character is a lady of the old school, full of the ideas which that school is vaguely supposed to entertain :—the rivalry between the judicial and the administrative, or "revenue," lines of the Service :—the contempt for non-official people, whom she classes indiscriminately as "interlopers" :—and a strong preference, (amounting in her case almost to a monomania,) for a permanent over an acting appointment. In Civilian parlance an employé who does vicarious duty for another is "cutcha," unless he be "confirmed" in his position, when he rises to the dignity of being "pucka," a word which denotes generally the perfect and the mature. Sucking Competition Wallahs may acquire from these pages some foretaste of Anglo-Indian slang : but they must be careful to bear in mind that the author is anything but a purist in Hindoostanee. The Dawk Bungalow was first acted at the residence of the Lieutenant-Governor of Bengal, before an audience nine-tenths of which held either pucka or cutcha appointments.

Dramatis Personæ.

Mr. JUDKINS, *Commissioner of Budgemahal.*
The Hon. Mr. HORACE CHOLMONDELEY, M.P., *a Gentleman travelling in search of facts.*
Lieut. MARSDEN, *of the* B.N.I., *Acting-Assistant-Sub-Deputy-Inspector of Bridges in the Public Works Department.*
ABDOOL, *a Madras Boy in the service of Mr.* CHOLMONDELEY.
The KHANSAUMAUN *or* STEWARD *of the Dawk Bungalow at Muckapore Bikra.*
Mrs. SMART, *Wife of the Judge of Budgemahal.*
Miss FANNY SMART, *her Daughter.*
SUSAN THACKER, *her European Lady's-maid.*

ACT I.

The Centre Room in the Dawk Bungalow at Muckapore Bikra.

A Bedstead and Table on opposite sides of the Apartment.

Enter CHOLMONDELEY *and* ABDOOL.

C.—Hi, there! Landlord! Landlord!

A.—Ho! Khansaumaun!　　　[*Enter* KHANSAUMAUN.

K.—Salaam, Sahib.

C.—Why didn't you come before, you lazy old rascal? Abdool, tell him to bring some soda-water.

A.—Ho, Khansaumaun—Belattee pawnee, brandy shrub!

C.—Abdool, let the landlord know that he had better make me comfortable. Tell him that I am an English gentleman of good family. Tell him, too, that I am related to the first Lord of the Admiralty.

A.—Ho, Khansaumaun! Sahib Burra Mahngee ke Bhai hai. Sahib Belattee koolin brahmin hai.*

K.—Bah Wah!

C.—Now I flatter myself that I have impressed him sufficiently. Abdool, ask him whether there are any letters for Mr. Cholmondeley.

A.—Chulmungular Sahib ke wasti chittee hi?

　　　　　　　[KHANSAUMAUN *gives a letter.*

C.—Here is a hand I ought to know. Why, it's from

---

* 'Ho, Khansaumaun! the Sahib is the brother of the great bargee.
'The Sahib is an English high-caste Brahmin.'

my old school-fellow Tom Blake, the Junior Secretary in the Home Department. Let me see what he says. [*Reads.*] 'Dear Chum, Very glad you enjoy your tour. Sorry I 'can't join you. My chief keeps me tight to work. Takes 'no holidays himself. Gives me fewer still.' Tom's style is curt. He is said to get through more work in a given time than any man in the secretariat; and, gad, I begin to understand how he earns his reputation. [*Reads*]—'I 'enclose a letter of introduction to old Judkins, the Com- 'missioner of Budgemahal. Tell you more about Waste 'Lands than any man in India. Wrote a report so long 'that the Lieutenant-Governor would not read it, and gave 'him Budgemahal to get him out of the way. Telegraphed 'to you on Friday week to say I would not come.' Hullo, Abdool, has a telegraph come for me?

A.—No, master. Master not understand Indian system of telegrumps. Suppose Blake Sahib want send telegrump to master, he send telegrump Friday. Next Monday he write letter. Master get letter first: tell him contents of telegrump. Two, three day after telegrump done coming. Master then know what to expect. That way no mistake made.

C.—O! that is the case, is it? I'll make a note of that in my commonplace-book. [*Writes*]—'Telegraph in India 'employed as auxiliary to epistolary communication.' Gad! I've neglected my commonplace-book lately. I must make up for lost time. But, while I think of it, let me settle my accounts. Abdool, what have you paid for me since yester-day morning?

A.—Master drive three dawks yesterday. Give syce three rupee, grass-cutter two rupee. Three syce three grass-cutter fifteen rupee. That make one gold mohur.

C.—That seems rather a high rate of tips, considering that the longest stage was under six miles.

A.—O, master plenty Burra Lord Sahib. Chota* Sahib one rupee give. Burra Sahib two rupee. Burra Lord Sahib three rupee.

C.—Well, the man's right. Gad, the man's right. But what did you pay at the bungalow where we stopped last night?

A.—Bungalow servants, three rupee yeight anna. Beer shrub, two rupee yeight anna. Master's bed, five rupee.

C.—Five rupees for the privilege of laying my mattress in an apartment shared by seven other individuals, where I was kept awake the first half of the night by two civilians discussing the respective merits of ryotwaree and village tenures, and the last half by two planters abusing the Secretary of State for India! Well, go on.

A.—Coolies, ten rupee.

C.—What! Ten rupees for carrying my baggage from the ghaut to the dog-cart?

A.—Master's bokkus plenty heavy. Wages plenty too much high. Coolies dig at Reproduckertive Pubberlic Workus. Coolie now get three rupee a day.

C.—Gad so. Very true. [*Writes*]—'Labour market 'sensibly understocked. Impulse given to trade by demand 'for cotton. Unskilled labour out here paid higher than 'skilled labour at home.' Go ahead.

A.—Light for cheroot, yeight anna. Master's dinner, twelve rupee.

C.—Why, I'd nothing but one curried fowl, and that fowl had no wings or breast. And, now that I come to

* Little.

think of it, the fowl I had the day before yesterday had no wings or breast either.   How's that, Abdool?

A.—Sahib, these Bengal fowls no wings got.   Bad fowl these.   Madras fowl plenty too much wings got.

C.—O, well, wings or no wings, I'm mortally tired of fowls.   I've had nothing for the last week but those unlucky birds, except, indeed, a pot of preserved grouse which had been left by an officer who was quartered in these parts during the mutiny.   [*Clucking heard outside.*]   What's that?

A.—Master's dinner done killing.

C.—O Lord! another fowl!   Well, what's the total of my account?

A.—Forty-nine rupee, twelve anna.

C.—Here's a fifty-rupee note.   Never mind the odd annas.   You may keep them for yourself.

A.—O, master very kind.   Plenty much thanks to master.   [*Exit* Cholmondeley *into Bedroom.*]   Ha! ha!— Master plenty wise Sahib.   He know plenty much about Indian institutions.   He not know greatest institution of all.   He never heard of dustoorie.*   Wah! Wah!   Here come one Burrah Mem Sahib, and one plenty pretty Missy Baba!   [*Enter* Mrs. Smart *and* Fanny, *followed by* Susan Thacker.]   Salaam, Lady!

F.—La, Ma, what a well-dressed bearer!   I wonder who he belongs to.

Mrs. S.—Kiska Nowkar?†

A.—My master Chulmungular Sahib.   Plenty great Sahib he.   Member of Council for making Laws and Regulations for Presidency of England.   [*Exit* Abdool.

---

* The commission pocketed by servants.

† 'Whose servant are you?'

Mrs. S.—Good gracious, Fanny, this must be Mr. Cholmondeley, the young Member of Parliament, about whom Mrs. Foley wrote to us from Calcutta. How fortunate we are in having met him here! Now listen, my dear! I insist on your making yourself agreeable to him. Don't frown, Miss. I *insist* upon it.

F.—I don't know what you mean by making myself agreeable, Ma. If I try to make myself more agreeable than Heaven made me, that would be flying in the face of Providence.

Mrs. S.—Silence, Fanny. Since that young Marsden came to the station your undutifulness has been past bearing. I wish he had been under the scaffolding when the roof of that new cutcherry which he was building fell in, and killed two mookhtars* and your Pa's principal Sudder Ameen.†

F.—How wicked of you to speak so, Mamma! I'm sure I don't know why you are always abusing that poor Mr. Marsden. I believe it's only because I care for him; and why shouldn't I care for him, I should like to know? [*Cries.*]

Mrs. S.—Why shouldn't you care for him, you abandoned girl? That I should live to hear *my* daughter ask such a question. Are you not aware, Fanny, that he is only *Acting*-Assistant-Sub-Deputy-Inspector? Do you imagine that I should give my child to a man whose appointment was not pucka?

F.—But, Mamma, is Mr. Cholmondeley's appointment pucka?

Mrs. S.—How can you talk such nonsense, child? One

---

* Attorneys.   † County Court Judge.

would think you only came out at the end of this cold
weather, instead of during the rains before last.   Mr.
Cholmondeley is a landed gentleman, and draws twelve
thousand rupees a month from his estates in Derbyshire,
besides holding Government paper to a large amount.

F.—Well, Ma, I don't see what that matters to us.   You
don't suppose he came to India to look for a wife?   He
might have found plenty of girls at home who would endure
to marry twelve thousand a month.

Mrs. S.—Choopraho!   You are a naughty, impertinent,
self-willed girl.   I have a good mind to counter-order the
Europe ball-dress which is coming out for you by the first
steamer in October.

F.—Why, Ma, you are always throwing that Europe
ball-dress in my teeth.   I hope and trust that before next
October I shall no longer depend upon you and Papa for
my wardrobe.

Mrs. S.—Well, Miss, if that means that you expect to
marry young Marsden—.   However, I'll have no more of
this.   But, Choop! Choop!   Somebody's coming.

Enter CHOLMONDELEY.

C.—Gad, what a pleasure there is in having a thorough
cleaning up after a journey!   I hate temporary measures.
None of your basins in the waiting-room, with a piece of
soap borrowed from the station-master, and a napkin abstracted from the refreshment buffet.   One never feels so
dirty as after a partial wash.   Ladies, by George!   [*Bows.*]
Madam, I fear that it was with the reverse of pleasure you
found a stranger already settled in the hotel.

Mrs. S.—O, sir, my daughter and I are much too old
travellers to expect solitude in a dawk bungalow.   As there

is no third party, I shall take the liberty of introducing myself as Mrs. Smart, wife of the late Judge of Budgemahal.

C. [*bows and writes.*]—'Peculiarities of Anglo-Indian 'manners. Old ladies take the liberty of introducing them-'selves as wives of the late Judge of Budgemahal.' Well, madam, since you have taken the initiative, allow me to present to your notice Mr. Horace Cholmondeley, of Paxton Park, Derbyshire.

Mrs. S.—Most happy, I am sure, to make your acquaintance.

C.—And, pray, who is the young lady with the bandbox?

Mrs. S.—That is our European lady's-maid, Mr. Cholmondeley.

C. [*aside.*]—A European lady's-maid! What gigantic ideas of nationality people have in this country! I suppose I shall hear next of a Caucasian cook and a Semitic footman.

Mrs. S.—This, Mr. Cholmondeley, is my daughter Fanny.

C.—My dear Mrs. Smart, your daughter? I thought she was your sister. [*Aside*]—Gad, I suspect I have offended the young lady more than I have pleased the old one. Miss Smart, I presume by your colour that you have only landed within the last month.

F.—Come, Mr. Cholmondeley, you can't return so soon upon your statement that I looked like my mother's sister. I came out during the rains before last, and two hot seasons have so altered me that I cannot wonder at strangers mistaking me for my own aunt.

C.—Two hot seasons! Good heavens, Miss Smart, what can the young men be about?

F.—Mr. Cholmondeley, the young men out here are

much too hardly worked to allow them time for paying impertinent compliments.   [*Walks across the stage.*

Mrs. S.—Mr. Cholmondeley, my daughter had a long dawk, and is tired and feverish.

C. [*bows and writes*]—'Peculiarities of Anglo-Indian 'manners.—When young ladies are rude they have had long dawks, and are tired and feverish.' I trust *you* have not suffered from the journey, Mrs. Smart?

Mrs. S.—No indeed. I am of the old school, Mr. Cholmondeley. These young ladies will dance till five o'clock in the morning for a week together, but a night in a palkee is too much for their delicate constitutions. Well do I remember how I came up-country with Mr. Smart to our first appointment five-and-twenty years ago. I landed at Garden Reach on the Monday, after a rapid passage of a hundred and sixty-four days in the 'Bombay Castle.' On the Wednesday I met Mr. Smart at a ball at the Chief's, and by Saturday evening we were in a budgerow on our way to Boglipore, which we reached after a pleasant voyage of seven weeks and three days. O, the delights of those days! My unwedded life in India was short indeed, for it extended only from the Monday evening till the Friday morning. But it was very sweet. I was acknowledged to be the belle of Calcutta; and a young gentleman was to have written me some verses in the *Friend of India*, but unfortunately I was married before the number came out. Ah, Mr. Cholmondeley! I was called the Europe Angel.

C.—Yes, the late Mr. Smart must have been indeed a happy man! You said the *late*, did not you? [*Sighs.*]

Mrs. S.—O no; not at all. I said the late Judge of Budgemahal. You must know, Mr. Cholmondeley, that a certain fatality has linked my husband's destiny to that of a person of the name of Judkins. Their rivalry dates from Haileybury, where Mr. Smart obtained seventeen gold and three silver medals, while Mr. Judkins was forced to content himself with three gold medals and seventeen silver. During the early part of their Indian career they were constantly pitted against each other. At length their lines diverged. Mr. Judkins went into the Revenue, and became Commissioner of Budgemahal; while my husband chose the Judicial, and was appointed to the judgeship at the same station. Mr. Cholmondeley, you will hardly believe the insults we endured for the last three years from that man and his low up-country-bred wife! Thank heaven, my husband has now risen in his own line out of reach of Mr. Judkins. He has been appointed within the last month to the Sudder Court* at Agra, and my daughter and I are now travelling down to join him. O, Mr. Cholmondeley! you little know the depth of villany to which a thorough-bred Revenue officer is capable of stooping.

C. [*writes*]—'Memo—To inform myself concerning the 'depth of villany to which a thorough-bred Revenue officer 'is capable of stooping.' I sympathise deeply, madam. Pray accept my warmest congratulations on your removal from the sphere of the machinations of that serpent. But what means of annoyance did he adopt?

Mrs. S.—Well, Mr. Cholmondeley, you must know that he has abetted a protegé of his own, one Marsden, who has paid his addresses to my daughter—a young man in the public works, who (would you believe it, Mr. Cholmondeley?) has not even been confirmed.

C.—The young heathen! And is not Mr. Marsden aware of his awful condition?

* The High Court.

Mrs. S.—No; extraordinary to relate, he shews the greatest indifference. And though he has plenty of interest, being, in fact, the son of a member of the Indian Council, he has not yet induced his father to use his influence to get him confirmed.

C.—Indeed! [*Writes*]—'The official element so strong 'out here that private influence is required to obtain the 'performance of the most ordinary rites of the church.' A new phase of nepotism, by George!

Mrs. S.—But, Mr. Cholmondeley, what has brought you into these parts?

C.—Well, my dear madam, I am on my way to the Sonepore meeting. I am told that I shall see more Indian life at the Sonepore Races in a week than during a year at Calcutta.

Mrs. S. [*with a bounce.*]—Indian life, indeed! A hole-and-corner gathering of Bahar people. I assure you, Mr. Cholmondeley, that we North-westers don't think so much of those down-country meetings. But to hear the Patna people talk, you would think Sonepore was the Derby and the St. Leger rolled into one. Indian life, indeed! Indian fiddlesticks!

C. [*aside.*]—Gad, the old girl seems irate. I'll go to my bedroom, and write out my notes. *Au revoir*, Mrs. Smart. I wish you good morning, Miss Smart.   [*Exit C.*

Mrs. S.—Well, Fanny, I hope you consider you have behaved rudely enough to Mr. Cholmondeley.

F.—O, Mamma, I cannot endure a swell, even though his whiskers are pucka; and, upon my honour, I believe that Mr. Cholmondeley's are only an acting pair.

Mrs. S.—How vulgar you are, Fanny! Why, Susan, what is the matter?

Susan.—Matter enough, ma'am! I have just seen with my own eyes young Mr. Marsden in the stable a-watching his horse having his gram, and smoking his cheroot as cool as if the bungalow belonged to him.

Mrs. S.—Horrid young man! How can he have the face to come across us? I am quite certain that odious Mr. Judkins cannot be far off. Whenever you see Mr. Marsden, you may be sure that his patron is somewhere in the neighbourhood.   [*Retires to rear of stage.*

Susan.—O, Miss, it is just what your Ma said, only I didn't dare to tell her so. That Mr. Judkins will be here in half-an-hour, and intends to stop till the cool of the evening. He is marching on a visit of inspection to the out-stations, to see that the roads are in proper order against the time that the members of Council go up to the Great Exhibition at Lahore. Mr. Marsden told me all that as free as might be, like a civil-spoken, handsome young gentleman as he is.

F.—Nonsense, Susan. But does Frank—does Mr. Marsden know that I—that our party is here?

Susan.—Yes, Miss. He said he knew it by the instinct of affection.

F.—He said a great deal of nonsense, I've no doubt. But silence. Here he comes.

Enter MARSDEN. *He goes up to* FANNY, *but* Mrs. SMART *steps in.*

Mrs. S.—Well, Mr. Marsden, I should have thought that you might have abstained from forcing yourself into our company during the last day we spend in this Division.

Before another word passes, I must insist on knowing definitely what are your intentions.

M.—My intentions, Mrs. Smart, are very avowable. I intend to have a bath and my tiffin, a smoke in the verandah, and possibly a peg,* or even two. I certainly have no desire to force myself into your company; but, unfortunately, the number of dawk bungalows at Muckapore Bikra is limited.

Mrs. S.—After what has passed, sir, you might have spared us the annoyance of this meeting.

M.—My dear Mrs. Smart, what can I do? You can hardly expect me to sit in the sun throughout the hottest hours in the day in this attitude. [*Squats down like a native.*] The villagers would mistake me for a Sahib who had turned Fakeer.

Mrs. S.—Sir, sir, I cannot stay here to be the butt of your ribaldry. I shall retire to my own apartment. As for you, Fanny, you may remain or not, as you like. But mind this : I absolutely forbid you to address a single word to this very objectionable young man. Do you hear, Miss?

F.—Yes, Mamma.

Mrs. S.—Do you heed, Miss?

F.—Yes, Mamma.   [*Exit* Mrs. Smart.

Fanny *sits down with her back to* Marsden ; Marsden *with his back to* Fanny.

M. [*aside*]—So we are not to address a single word to each other, ar'n't we? Well, thank Heaven! no one can forbid us to soliloquise. [*Aloud.*] I wonder what Mrs. Smart meant by talking about this being her last day in the Division.

---

* The Anglo-Indian slang for brandy and soda-water.

F.—Susan, I wish Papa had not been appointed to that horrid Agra. To think that I have seen dear, dear Budge-mahal for the last time !

M. [*jumping up*]—Good heavens ! What do I hear? The Smarts leaving Budgemahal ! What a frightful blow to my hopes ! By Jove ! sooner than such a misfortune should befal me, I would consent to give up my appointment, and enter the Staff Corps. 'Pon honour I would.

F.—And to think of the pleasant months we passed there ! The pic-nics ! The balls ! The ho-o-o-g-hunting parties ! [*Cries.*] O Susan, I am so wretched.

M.—Heavens ! what a fool I was not to yield to Mrs. Smart's wishes, and get my father to ask Strachey to confirm me in my appointment !

F. [*cries*]—O me ! O me ! How I do hate that word p-p-pucka ! I wish all the pucka appointments in the country were at the bottom of the sea.

M.—I cannot bear this. Fanny ! [FANNY *shakes her head.*] Dearest Fanny ! how can you be so cruel as not to vouchsafe one word at this our last meeting? And yet why should it be our last meeting? [*Aside.*] I have it. [*Aloud.*] Hem ! I should not wonder if Mrs. Smart's bearers were to strike work to-morrow morning, opposite the mango-tope, beyond the eighth mile-stone on the Agra road. These fellows are so insolent with unprotected females. How fortunate it is that our camp is pitched in this precise tope ! Mrs. Smart and Fanny will have some-where to shelter themselves during the heat of the day. By Jove ! I'll go at once and warn the bearers that they had better not strike work to-morrow morning, opposite the mango-tope, beyond the eighth mile-stone on the Agra road.

[*Exit* MARSDEN.

F.—O, I cannot, cannot part from him! O, Mamma, how could you be so cruel?

Susan.—Well, miss, I don't wonder you're so fond of him.   He is such a sweet young man, though he is cutcha. Thank goodness, my young man's pucka, though he is only a subordinate Government Salt Chowkie.   However, he has great hopes of being promoted to be an opium godown.

Enter JUDKINS.

J.—Miss Smart! Dear me, Miss Smart, I am very fortunate in meeting you once more before you leave my division.   Budgemahal will long regret the loss of its fairest flower.

F.—O, Mr. Judkins, I am so glad to see you again. You have been always so kind to me.

J.—Glad to see me again, eh, Miss Fanny?   I suppose that there are others of your family here who will not be equally enchanted?   Eh?

F.—Come, Mr. Judkins, you must not make jokes about Mamma.   But,—O, how shall I ever thank you enough for —for—for—   .

J.—For doing my best to smooth matters with reference to a certain young gentleman?   Is that what you mean? Eh, Fanny?   Well, what should you say if I told you I had written a private note to my good friend, the Lieutenant-Governor of the North-West, telling him exactly how the matter stands; and, from what I know of Drummond, I'll engage that we shall have some good news in a day or two. He always had a soft heart, had Drummond.   So, if Frank is confirmed, he will owe it to you, and nobody but you; eh, Fanny?

F.—O, Mr. Judkins, how could you?   You unkind,

treacherous, inconsiderate—dear old friend! God bless you. [*Kisses him and runs out.*

J.—Well, she's a darling girl. It is hard to say whether she takes less after her father or mother. Smart was the greatest fool among the Zillah Judges, and now will be the greatest fool in the Sudder Court; while the mother—— But I don't trust myself to speak about the mother. [*Enter* MARSDEN.] Well, youngster, have you seen to the horses? How the Arab's off fore-leg?

M.—No better than it should be, I'm afraid.

J.—You've ordered dinner, I suppose. What's the bill of fare?

M.—Oh, the usual thing. Sub kooch hai, Sahib.* Muttony chop nahin hai. Beefy-steak nahin hai. Unda bakun nahin hai. Ducky stew nahin hai. Moorghee grill hai. [*A fowl runs across the stage, with* KHANSAUMAUN *in pursuit. Soft music.*]

Enter CHOLMONDELEY.

M.—Hallo, Mr. Judkins, here's Lord Dundreary; or at any rate his brother Sam, come out in the Uncovenanted Service.

C.—Haw! Haw! Have I the pleasure of addressing the Commissioner of Budgemahal?

J.—You have, Sir.

C.—Will you then allow me to present you with a letter of introduction from Mr. Blake, Junior Secretary of the Home Department?

J.—I shall be most delighted to serve in any way a friend of Tom's. I never came across so promising a subordinate. Ah, Marsden, you would do well to tread in

* Anything you like, Sahib.

his steps. [*Reads.*] So it appears, Mr. Cholmondeley, that you want to be put up to a thing or two about Waste Lands. Well, though I say it as shouldn't, you could not well have applied to a better man. Could he, Frank? Now, I'll tell you how we'll set to work. You shall commence your acquaintance with the subject by reading my celebrated Minute to the Lieutenant-Governor, which procured me my present appointment. It will give you a good general view of the subject in a small compass. It is a mere sketch. Perhaps about half again as long as Mr. Plowden's Salt Report.

C.—Why, my good Sir, Mr. Plowden's Report served me for reading all the way from Marseilles to the Sand-heads, and then I had only got into Henry Meredith Parker's letters.

J.—Well, well, I'll point out the passages best worth reading. And then, when you have mastered the outlines, we'll go into the details. Tell you what! If you'll join my camp for a week or so, you will have the opportunity of hearing my decision in several most important cases. We'll make you very comfortable, and perhaps we may manage to shew you a little hog-hunting.

C.—O, Sir, you are very good; very good, indeed, 'pon honour. I shall accept your invitation with great pleasure; that is to say, if it does not incommode you.

J.—Incommode me! Who ever heard of incommoding in India? Unfortunately, we have only one spare tent, and that is a fly: unless, indeed, you care to double up with Frank. Well, I must go and make myself decent. I'll leave you with Marsden. [*Exit.*

M.—May I ask what has brought you to India, Mr. Cholmondeley? Did you come out for sport, eh?

C.—Well, Mr. Marsden, I came out in search of facts : in quest of political capital, Mr. Marsden.   During my first week I went about incognito, under the idea that people would speak more freely with an obscure Mr. Smith than they would venture to do in the presence of a member of the English Legislature ; but I found that I was generally mistaken for the commercial traveller of a leading military tailor in Dhurrumtollah,* to whom I happened to bear a casual resemblance.   In consequence, I could not obtain the *entrée* of civilian society, and was forced to confine myself to the information which could be picked up in the dawk bungalows.   Now, the political creed of the frequenters of dawk bungalows is too uniform to afford a field for the minute observer ; for it consists in the following tenets—that the Modified Resolutions are the curse of the country ; that Sir Mordaunt Wells is the greatest judge that ever sat on the English bench ; and that when you hit a nigger he dies on purpose to spite you.

M.—So you ceased to call yourself Smith?

C.—Yes, I ceased to call myself Smith, and adopted the title of Captain Jones, of the 4th Madras Native Infantry, travelling up-country to do duty with a Sikh regiment at Peshawur.   Thenceforth I lived exclusively in military society.

M.—Well, did you get on better than before?

C.—No, begad, I found that the political creed of the mess-rooms was even more simple than that of the dawk bungalows ; for it was confined to one article of faith, which appeared to include all others—that since the Amalgamation the Service had gone to the devil.

---

* Dhurrumtollah is the Bond-street of Calcutta, as Chowringhee is its Belgravia.

M.—So now you're travelling in your own character?

C.—Yes. In my character of member of the English Legislature I go where I like, am welcome everywhere, and obtain information from persons of all shades of opinion. Ah! I've heard some facts which never come to the ears of you civilians. You think you know India, but, after all, you take good care to hear only what suits your book. I could tell you stories that would make you stare.

M.—Could you give me a specimen, Mr. Cholmondeley?

C.—Well, it was only yesterday that I was dining at the house of an indigo planter, and he told me the following anecdote, which I am assured is well authenticated. A friend of his was desirous of purchasing some waste land which lay between the estates of two native Zemindars. He offered the Commissioner a certain sum of money; and these two native fellows subscribed, and offered a larger: and (would you believe it?) the Commissioner actually accepted their bid.

M.—Good heavens! It is almost incredible.

C.—Ah! You civilians see only one side of the question. Wait till I take my seat again in the Commons House of Parliament. Wait till I rise in my place, and stand on the floor of the House, and say, 'Sir, when from the top of the 'Ochterlony Monument I looked down on the environs of 'the capital of India; when I saw her stately river crowded 'with sails, her wharfs heaped with bales and casks, her 'network of railways bearing the products of her industry to 'every corner of that vast continent, from Barrackpore to 'Diamond Harbour, from Budge-Budge to Dum-Dum;— 'then, Sir, I am free to confess that I took a solemn vow to 'exert my every power for the great principle of the De- 'velopment of the Resources of India.'

[*Knocks down the punkah. Enter* ABDOOL.

M.—Hear! hear! That will have a grand effect in the House of Commons. Only I doubt whether they have any punkahs there.

C. [*very much excited*]—I assure you that you civilians know nothing about the country. [*Takes a chair, and sits astride opposite* MARSDEN.]—Look at the railways alone, Sir ! What a field for the efforts of an enlightened Government ! Connect Benares with Allahabad, connect Agra with Delhi, and what results will follow ! The stream of passengers will flow up to the Punjab—[*Hits* MARSDEN'S *knee one way*].

M.—Don't, Sir !

C.—And down to the Lower Gangetic provinces ! [*Hits it the other way.*]

M.—Have done, will you ?

C.—Our silver will pour from West to East ! [*Hits* MARSDEN'S *knee again.*]

M.—Confound you, Sir !

C.—The produce of the looms of Cabul and the gorgeous fabrics of Cashmere will pour from East to West. [*In attempting the same manœuvre, he overbalances the chair and tumbles over.*]

M. [*picking him up*]—Holloa ! There appears to have been a collision on the line. I hope the gorgeous fabrics of Cashmere are not damaged.

C. [*confused, and rubbing his leg*]—Ah ! you civilians know nothing about the country.

M.—But, my good Sir, I'm not a civilian.

C.—Well then, Sir, you ought to be. You ought to be, if you're not. Sir, I wish you a very good morning.

[*Exit* CHOLMONDELEY.

A.—Master plenty excitable Sahib. Whenever master done say ' Develeropment of Soorces of India,' then he talk plenty much and get plenty angry. I sing you song 'bout master. [*Sings.*]

> My master is a great Sahib,
>   With whiskers fine and long,
> And on a public question
>   He comes out very strong.
> Judge Campbell of the High Court,
>   And Mr. Seton Karr,
> Whene'er they see my master
>   Invite him from afar :

' Walk in, Chumley, walk in, Chumley, pray,
' Walk into the High Court, this warm and sunny day ;
' Walk into the High Court, this afternoon so fine,
' And listen to my reasoning on Ten of Fifty-nine."*

M.—Well, you are a droll fellow. Who taught *you* to sing English tunes?

A.—Missionary Sahib teach me to sing down Madras way. I learn plenty too many hymn tunes in Mission School. I Christian boy, master.

M.—Oh, you're a Christian, are you?

A.—Yes, Sahib, I Christian boy. Plenty poojah† do Sunday time. Never no work do. Plenty wrong that.

M.—No. I 'll be bound you appreciate that part of our religion. Well, whatever your tenets may be, you are a funny dog. Here 's a rupee for you.

A.—O, master too good : plenty too much good. I sing 'nother song to master :—

---

* Act Ten of 1859 embodied a most praiseworthy effort to grapple with the rent question—a matter too serious to be discussed in the note to a farce.

† Religious worship.

The Judge and the Collector
　They both have gone away,
Gone to Mussoorie
　Their Privilege Leave to stay :
And, while they're off together
　On a little bit of spree,
I 'm off to Sonepore
　The Planters' Cup to see.

Old Jones my chief descried me.
　Says he : ' I greatly grieve
' To see you here at Sonepore
　' Without my special leave.'
Says I : ' I ventured hither
　' To come, Sir, in the hope
' Of playing croquet with Miss Jones
　' Beneath the race-course tope.'

Enter JUDKINS.

J.—Hollo, Marsden, you appear to be having a tumasha*
here on your own account.   If it's all the same to you, I 'll
assume the liberty of sending this fellow about his business
(if he has got any, that is to say, which doesn't seem probable) and taking a quiet snooze.   Jao !†   [*Exit* ABDOOL.]
Wake me when dinner comes, there 's a good boy.   [*Goes
to sleep, with a handkerchief over his face.*]

M.—Well, what with that Madras boy and his master,
I don't know when I have spent a more amusing time in
a dawk bungalow.   But I wish Fanny would come out
again.   If she has half the sense I give her credit for, she

---

* A musical or theatrical entertainment.　　† Be off !

ı

will find out that the coast is clear, and take her opportunity. I 'll run the risk, and tap at her door.   No ; excellent idea ! I 'll let off the cork of a bottle of Belattee pawnee against the panel, and then, if the mother comes out instead of Fanny, I can pretend that it was done by mistake.   [*Takes a bottle of soda-water, and lets off the cork.*]

Enter FANNY.

F.—My dear Mr. Marsden, how very rash you are ! How could you knock at our door ?

M.—I protest, Fanny, that your suspicions are unworthy of you.   I was making the preparations for a modest peg, when out you bolt, and charge me in the most gratuitous manner with knocking at your door.   Knocking at the door ! Do you take me for a species of Anglo-Indian old Joe ?   I assure you I feel your conduct deeply.   [*Turns away.*]

F.—Well, well, Frank, I beg your pardon for my suspicions, though I cannot help thinking that they are not without foundation.   But have you nothing pretty to say to me, now I am here ?

M.—Nothing except what I 've told you a thousand times already, that you are the dearest, sweetest of women ; that you are a pucka angel ; that I would die for you ; that I would give up my accumulated arrears of privilege leave for you ; that for you I would do unpaid duty with the East Indian Regiment at Dacca.   In fact, everything that I have told you so often and so eagerly ever since that thrice auspicious night (you remember it, Fanny ?) when the Station Ball was held in the Judge's Cutcherry, much to the disgust of your respected Governor.   Shall you ever forget how we pulled a cracker together, and how I read to you the motto—simple verses, perhaps, Fanny, but dearer to me thenceforward than all Shakspeare, and Tennyson, and Byron bound up together?

> ‘ I soon shall die unless I see
> That you love me as I love thee;
> For ’tis for you alone I live,
> And nought but that can pleasure give.’

F.—Well, well! I won’t deny that we have talked a great deal of pleasant nonsense together. But I have a piece of news for you. Are you sure he’s asleep? [JUDKINS *snores.*]

M.—He’s not very wide awake at any rate.

F.—Dear old gentleman! Would you believe it, Frank? He has written a private letter to Mr. Drummond, telling him our whole story, and requesting that your appointment may be confirmed.

M.—Has he indeed? What a jolly old budzart it is!

F.—But listen, Frank. The answer has not come yet, and before it arrives we shall be at Agra, and you far away at some out-station making horrid bridges that will all tumble down next rainy season. Ah me! What an unlucky girl I am!

M.—No, you are not, Fanny. An unlucky girl never has a devoted lover with hopes of a pucka appointment. I don’t intend that you shall leave the district until Mr. Drummond’s answer comes. Don’t you remember that I expressed to you my apprehension lest your bearers should strike work opposite the mango-tope beyond the eighth mile-stone on the Agra road; in which case your mother and you would be forced to take shelter in our camp? Well! That apprehension has since been converted into a horrible certainty.

F.—Good heavens, Frank, do you mean to say that you have bribed the bearers?

M.—There ! There ! Don't speak so loud ! Think on the enormity of the misdemeanour you have imputed to me. What would the *Englishman* say if it heard that an English official had been instigating natives to violate a contract after receiving a consideration ? Conceive the tone of the leading article that would infallibly be written. ' It is con-' fidently asserted that a young gentleman in the Public ' Works Department, who, though not a civilian himself, ' has been so long under civilian influence as to be imbued ' with the traditional policy of the class, has, in virtue of his ' high authority, used underhand means to induce the palkee-bearers'——Good heavens, here's your mother ! [*They start apart.*]

Enter Mrs. SMART.

Mrs. S.—What do I see ? Fanny, have you no delicacy, no retenue ? If I turn my back for ten minutes you disobey my positive orders, throw to the winds my maternal au-thority, and openly encourage the advances of an *acting* officer. And you, Sir—do you consider it manly to pre-sume on the unfortunate chance which has thrown you once more of necessity into our society ? You allow me no choice. I must throw myself on the protection of the other visitors at the bungalow. Here is one asleep on a chair. Whoever he is, he has the heart of an Englishman, and will not see me insulted by a profligate : and, what is more, a profligate who is not even pucka. Sir, I appeal to you. [*Twitches the handkerchief off* JUDKINS' *face, who rises, and confronts her.*] Mr. Judkins ! So you are the person who has arranged a meeting for these two young people to come off under your auspices ! So you are the go-between in this precious love-affair ! So this match is to be of your making! So, Mr. Judkins, after robbing me and Mr. Smart of our peace, you intend to rob us of our daughter!

J.—Good gracious, Mrs. Smart, I have no idea what you are driving at. All I know about the matter is that I was enjoying a very sweet dream, and that I have awoke to an exceeding unpleasant reality.

Mrs. S. [*curtsies*]—O, Mr. Judkins, you are pleased to be sarcastic. Would you however, if you can for a few moments rein in your satire, tell me in plain words why you thought fit to sanction by your presence an interview between my daughter and a young man of whom you know well I disapprove?

J.—Well, Mrs. Smart, I can only repeat that I was aroused from a slumber such as only the innocent can enjoy to find myself in the presence of two people looking very shy, and one looking very angry. That is all the part I have had in the affair. Not that I should have objected to play Friar Lawrence to so dashing a Romeo and so sweet a Juliet. [*Bows to* FANNY.]

Mrs. S.—Well, upon my word, Mr. Judkins! Upon my word! Perhaps you won't call a daughter of mine names, though she has descended below herself on this occasion.

J.—After all, Mrs. Smart, I am surprised that you do not consider your daughter honoured by the attentions of so fine a young fellow.

Mrs. S.—Mr. Judkins, *I* have principles. It is not for nothing that I trace my origin on either side from old Indian families. I thank heaven that *I* have been brought up to know the difference between pucka and cutcha appointments.

J.—I have no doubt you do, Mrs. Smart; I have no doubt you do; and I have no doubt either that when you retire from the service Sir Charles Wood will at once offer you a seat in the Indian Council.

Mrs. S.—That, I suppose, would be considered wit at the Board of Revenue :—a Board of which you doubtless count upon becoming the most brilliant light. You are an ornament to your line of the service, Mr. Judkins; you are indeed.

J.—My line ! Bless the woman ! My line ! Well, whatever it may be, I cannot say it has at present fallen to me in a pleasant place.

Enter SUSAN, *with tray.   Sets it down on table.*

Susan.—Never mind him, ma'am.   I 've made a nice basin of soup for you and Miss Fanny.   After your long journey you won't be right again till you 've had something to eat.

Mrs. S.—Well, Mr. Judkins, I am sorry that I so far forgot myself as to address you.   Come, Fanny, and take your tiffin.   Thank heaven, it is the last meal we shall eat in the same room with the present company.   (*Mrs.* SMART *and* FANNY *sit down at the table.*]

Enter KHAUSAUMAUN *with dinner.*

K.—Khana tyar hi, Sahib.*

J.—Khansaumaun, palanpur khana rucko.†   Come, Marsden, we must rough it a little to accommodate the ladies. [*Aside.*]   Horrid old woman !   I should like to accommodate her into the middle of next week.   [JUDKINS *and* MARSDEN *sit down at the bed.*]   Marsden, I feel a little

---

* 'Dinner is ready, Sahib.'

† 'Steward, put the dinner on the bed.'

out of sorts. A cup of tea might do us both good. Ho, Khansaumaun! Chah banno !*

Mrs. S.—Well, I never! Tea for tiffin! What would an official of the good old school say if he heard a Mofussil Commissioner ordering tea for tiffin? Tea, indeed! Ho, Khansaumaun, beer shrub lao !

J.—This moorghee is plaguy tough. Ho, Khansaumaun, aur kooch hai ?†

K.—Sahib, curry bat hai.

J.—Oh, bother curry bat! It's only the old moorghee under another shape. We'll have some eggs with our tea. Ho, Khansaumaun, unda lao, toast banno.

Mrs. S.—Tea, toast, and boiled eggs! There's a tiffin for a Covenanted Servant of five-and-twenty years' standing ! Fancy a Senior Merchant‡ going without his curry bat. Ho ! curry bat do !

J.—Well, I should have thought that the temper of some people was hot enough already without requiring to be warmed by curry.

Mrs. S.—Fanny, I repent more and more having been betrayed into an altercation with that man. However, I am resolved never to address another word to him.

J.—For these and all his mercies make us truly thankful !

Mrs. S. [*starts up*]—What is that, Sir? What is this last piece of insolence to which you have given vent?

J. [*without turning*]—I was only saying grace after meat, or rather after moorghee.

Mrs. S.—Your brutality, Sir, is only equalled by your impiety.

---

* 'Make some tea.'   † 'Is there anything else ?'

‡ In days gone by the Company's servants were classed as Senior Merchants, Junior Merchants, and Writers.

J.—Pray sit down, Mrs. Smart.   I have no intention of betraying you into a second altercation.

Mrs. S. [sits down].—Monster !   Fanny, would that we were out of this dreadful place !

J.—The agreeableness of places generally depends on the state of our tempers.   For my part, this bungalow seems quite a paradise.   Thank Providence for having endowed me with an imperturbable tranquillity !

Mrs. S.—Hem !   Fanny, did you hear what your papa said to the Lieutenant-Governor about the inefficiency of Revenue officers when concerned with a question of law ? He told Mr. Drummond that during the past year, in a certain division, there was not one in ten of the Commissioner's decisions which would not have been reversed before the most ordinary tribunal.

J. [starts up]—To what division did he refer, Mrs. Smart ?   If he alluded to Budgemahal, he was knowingly guilty of a vile calumny.

Mrs. S. [without turning]—Pray sit down, Mr. Judkins. I have no desire of being betrayed into a second altercation.

J.—Mrs. Smart, whoever uttered that falsehood was capable of anything : even of marrying a low, uneducated, up-country-bred wife.

Mrs. S. [starts up]—Mr. Judkins, my father enjoyed the highest judicial appointments in the Covenanted Service ; and my dear mother was grand-daughter of the first judge of the first settled district in Bengal, Behar, and Orissa. No member of our family ever dabbled in Revenue.

J.—Ha !   Ha !   Ha !   My dear Mrs. Smart, your mother's brother ended his career as Sub-collector of Shahabad ; and devilish glad he was to get the appointment.

Mrs. S.—Go on, Mr. Judkins ; pray go on.   Thank

heaven, *I* was brought up among people who knew the difference between pucka and cutcha appointments.

J.—Mrs. Smart, the last place which your father held was that of Acting Magistrate at Jessore :—*Acting* Magistrate, do you hear, Mrs. Smart?

Mrs. S.—Base man, you never uttered a more contemptible slander :—a slander worthy of one who gained his present position by acting as stalking-horse to his Lieutenant-Governor.

J.—Mrs. Smart! Who schemed to get the Governor-General's Aide-de-Camp for her daughter?

Mrs. S.—Mr. Judkins! Who refused to subscribe to the new church on the pretext that the padre was a humbug?

J.—Who asked the Station to dinner, and allowed only one glass of simkin* to each guest—eh, Mrs. Smart?

Mrs. S.—Who tried to lead off the District Ball, and didn't know his steps—eh, Mr. Judkins?

[*They both speak at once. Curtain falls.*

ACT II.

Outside the Commissioner's Tent. Table and Chairs at one side of the Stage.

Enter JUDKINS *from tent, in dressing-gown.*

J.—Well! I'm all the better for a good night. I always manage to sleep sound in camp. Now for a bath. Ho, Bheestie!† This is a very pleasant camping ground, but

---

* Champagne. † Bath-man.

I wonder why Marsden insisted so strongly on our stopping here instead of going on to Bunderbustgunge. Whatever I said, he would have it that there was nothing like the mango tope just beyond the eighth mile-stone on the Agra Road. The eighth mile-stone on the Agra Road! Young men are not, generally speaking, so accurate about the number of their mile-stones. However, he's a dear boy, and I always humour him. [*Enter* MARSDEN.] I say, young shaver, what makes you so particular about the eighth mile-stone on the Agra Road? I wish now that we had pushed on to Bunderbustgunge.

M.—Well, my dear Sir, I'll make a confession. You must know that I have received information which leads me to suppose that Mrs. Smart's bearers will strike work somewhere near this spot.

J.—You have received information which leads you to suppose! You unscrupulous young villain! Well! I presume that you intend to saddle me with the women for the rest of the day?

M.—Such, I blush to say, is my intention. Now, my dear Sir, will you do me a great—a very great favour? Will you be very civil to Mrs. Smart? [JUDKINS *shakes his head.*] For my sake and for Fanny's, Mr. Judkins!

J.—Well! well! the woman will be out of the country in another day. I promise to be as polite to her as she will allow me to be. But here's the bheestie.

Enter BHEESTIE *with water-skin. Exeunt* JUDKINS *and* BHEESTIE *into tent.*

M.—Now for the pleasantest hour of the twenty-four. Ho, Sirdar! Chah lao!* [*Enter* CHOLMONDELEY, *in hunt-*

* 'Bring my tea.'

ing costume, followed by ABDOOL.]　The top of the morning to you, Mr. Cholmondeley.

C.—Fine morning this. [*Aside.*] What a damned foolish observation ! It always is a fine morning in India.

M.—Are you ready for some chota hazaree ?*

C.—Chota hazaree ! What 's chota hazaree ?

M.—Why, the meal I 'm taking at the present moment.

C.—O, begad ! They call that down in Madras 'early tea.' So 'chota hazaree' is 'early tea.'

M.—Just so. 'Chota,' 'early'; 'hazaree,' 'tea.'

C.—O ! 'Chota' is 'early,' is it? Well, that accounts for the assistant-magistrate being termed the Chota Sahib. He gets up early to go to Cutcherry,† while the collector lies in bed to wait till the appeals come in. I 'll put that down. [*Writes.*]

M.—You 've hit it. But here come the papers. What an old brick Judkins is for taking in such a packet of them ! The *Hurkaru* as usual. An article comparing Sir Charles Wood to Nero, and Sir Mordaunt Wells to Aristides. Very pretty reading for rabid Anglo-Saxons ! And here 's the *Delhi Punch!* I did hope we had marched out of the region within which circulates that melancholy periodical. After all, there 's nothing like the *Englishman.* What 's the news, Cholmondeley? [*Sips his tea.*]

C.—Let 's see. [*Reads.*] 'Latest from America.—The 'Federals under Meade attacked Lee's position on the 'morning of the 18th, and after three days' hard fighting 'were forced to recross the Rappahannock after losing 'fifteen thousand men.' 'Latest from Furruckabad.—There 'is no truth in the report that Lieutenant Smith, of the

* Literally, 'little breakfast.'　　† Court.

'Engineers, is about to avail himself of some days' leave.'
H'm! h'm! h'm!   [*Splashing heard inside the tent.*

M.—There's the old boy having his mussuck.*

C. [*reads.*]—'The *Nubia* arrived at Garden Reach on
'the 12th instant. Passengers—Mr. Williams, B.C.S.,
'Captain James, B.N.I., Mrs. James, Miss Prettyman.'
H'm! h'm! h'm! 'Married, on the 15th instant, at the
'Cathedral, John Williams, collector and magistrate of
'Mozufferpore, to Alicia, eleventh daughter of the late
'Ebenezer Prettyman of the Bengal Civil Service.' Quick
work that—eh, Mr. Marsden?

M.—Oh, nothing out of the way. But might I ask why
you are got up in that style?

C.—I'm going out for my first day's hog-hunting. [*Enter*
JUDKINS.] Good morning, Mr. Judkins. I'm off to cover
side.

J.—Well, let me give you a piece of advice. Don't you
go mistaking tame pigs for wild. If you see a fellow with
a straight tail, whip him through the body; but if you come
across a curly-tailed chap, fight shy of him. He's being fed
up for the Agricultural Exhibition at Alipore. But the sun
is getting powerful, and I must be going inside the tent.
I wish you good sport.   [*Exit* JUDKINS *into tent.*

M.—Good-bye, Cholmondeley. Don't forget; the wild
pigs have curly tails. Curly tails, remember! You'll get
into no end of trouble if you kill a fellow with a straight
tail.   [*Exit* MARSDEN.

A.—Master plenty great shikaree.† Master go kill
plenty pig. I stay 'tome. Make good master's clothes.

C.—Yes. You stay at home, Abdool. Have some

---

* Water-skin.   † Sportsman.

coffee ready for me when I come back. Take care of my things.

A. [*aside.*]—Ha! ha! I take care of master's spirit chest. Cognac shrub, plenty nice drink. I got no caste. I plenty good Christian. Drink plenty rum. Do no work Sunday. Them my Thirty-nine Article-icle-icles.

[*Exit* ABDOOL.

C.—Now I'll be off. Holloa! What the deuce is the row now? Here's the European lady's-maid.

Enter SUSAN.

Susan.—O! thank goodness, here's a belattee Christian man! O, Sir! O, Mr. Chimbly! Here's such a dreadful business!

C.—Why, bless my soul, young woman, what ever is the matter?

Susan.—Why, Sir—would you believe it?—as soon as ever we came opposite that there mangel-wurzel tope the bearers put down the palkees with a bang, and cut and run into the jungle. O my poor mistress! My poor mistress!

Enter Mrs. SMART *and* FANNY.

Mrs. S.—O, dear me, Fanny, what shall we do? I never was in such a position. Here we are in the full heat of the sun, four coss from the last dawk bungalow, and the Lord only knows how many from the next.

F.—Yes, Mamma, what shall we do? O! What could have induced the bearers to behave so? [*Pretends to cry.*

Mrs. S.—Bless my heart, there's Mr. Cholmondeley. O! Mr. Cholmondeley, I am so glad to see you. Those budmashes* who were carrying our palkees have run away

* Mauvais sujets.

into the tope. We had only three coss to go, and we should have met a pair of tum-tums* which would have taken us on to the Grand Trunk Road, where my husband was to have met us with the two-horse gharee.† I had made such an utcha bunderbust.‡

C.—My dear Madam! My dear Madam! Are you sure you perceive the full extent of your misfortune? I am convinced that there is more in this than you think. Mere ryots would never have arrived at such a pitch of insolence unless they had been aware that a mutiny was imminent. We are on the eve of another outbreak. Did you observe whether the men called out 'Deen! Deen!'§ as they ran into the jungle?

Mrs. S.—Good heavens, Mr. Cholmondeley, how should Hindoo ryots call out 'Deen! Deen!' I should as soon expect to meet Dr. Pusey walking up and down the High Street of Oxford, bawling out 'No Popery!'

C.—Now, Mrs. Smart, do be advised, and make a timely retreat. At such a crisis hesitation is death. Allow me to conduct you to the nearest military station. I will hold Miss Smart before me on the horse's neck, while you ride on the crupper with your arms round my waist.

Mrs. S.—Ride to the nearest military station with my arms round your waist! Why, people would think we were the last elopement from Simla.

C.—We will pursue our way at night. You shall hide in the jungle during the day, and I will repair to the neighbouring villages disguised as a fakeer.

Mrs. S.—Nonsense, Sir. You won't find it so easy to frighten an old Mofussil lady. The truth of the matter is

* Dog-carts.　　† Carriage.　　‡ Excellent arrangement.
§ 'The Faith! The Faith!' The rallying cry of the Mahommedans.

that I was foolish enough to pay these budmashes before-hand, and they have thrown me over. I must have been an idiot to do it!

C.—O, that quite alters the business, Mrs. Smart. This is a clear case of Wilful Breach of Contract. 'Pon honour, Mrs. Smart, I believe it comes within the scope of the clauses of Mr. Maine's new Bill.

Mrs. S.—Well, I dare say it does: but I don't see how that will help us: unless, indeed, Mr. Maine would go into the next village and beat up for coolies. But what do you advise, Mr. Cholmondeley?

C.—Well, Mrs. Smart, I should advise you to institute a civil suit at once; and, meanwhile, I will press the Government at home to pass a modified Criminal Contract Bill. I will engage to do that much for you, Mrs. Smart.

Mrs. S.—Bless me, Sir, if you have no wiser suggestion to make you had better choop. A modified Criminal Contract Bill, indeed!

C.—Well, it appears that I can't be of much use in this quarter. I shall mount and be off. Good-bye, Mrs. Smart. Good-bye, Miss Smart. [*Aside.*] Let me see! The tame pig has a straight tail, and the wild pig a curly tail. I'll take good care to keep that in my head.

[*Exit* CHOLMONDELEY.

Mrs. S.—Well, Fanny, there's an ooloo-ke-butcha* for you. He'll never set the Hooghly on fire. I wish we could see some sensible, good-natured man who knows the country. Dear me! What with the heat and vexation, I am quite overcome. I never was out in the sun so late before. Dear me! What ever shall I do? [*Cries.*] I wish somebody would come to our assistance. What would I

* Son of an owl.

give to see a civilian,—or—a military man,—or—or—or—
an uncovenanted servant, or—or—or—or—or—or—an in-
terloper.

Enter MARSDEN.

M.—What do I see? Mrs. Smart, and in tears! I
hope and trust no accident has happened to your party.
Can I be of any service to you?

Mrs. S.—Oh, Sir, we are in great trouble on account of
the dishonesty of our bearers, who have taken to their heels
and left the palkees In the middle of the road some hundred
yards from hence.

M.—Dear me! I am very much concerned. What a
set of rascals! I trust, Madam, that you have received no
injury.

Mrs. S. [*aside*]—Upon my word he is a very polite
young man. I begin to wish he was pucka. [*Aloud.*] No,
Sir, we have received no injury, but a great deal of in-
convenience. We have still three coss to travel before we
reach the tum-tums.

M.—Oh, in that case, pray do not trouble yourself. I
shall have great pleasure in driving you on your way in our
gharee : that is to say, if you will permit me to have the
honour of so doing.

Mrs. S. [*aside*]—He certainly is most courteous. I *do*
wish he was pucka. [*Aloud.*] Oh, Sir, many, many thanks.
Under the circumstances, I shall have great pleasure in ac-
cepting your very kind offer.

M.—I am sure, Mrs. Smart, yourself and your daughter
must have been much shaken by this *contretemps.* Would
you do us the honour of taking some rest and refreshment
in the tent?

Mrs. S. [*aside*]—He is really a delightful young man. I begin not to care whether he is pucka or cutcha. [*Aloud.*] Sir, I am deeply obliged to you, but I cannot consent to receive the hospitality of Mr. Judkins. I prefer remaining here. [*Opens her umbrella.*]

M. [*sighs*]—Ah, Madam, you little know how deeply wounded would be the heart of that gentleman could he hear the sentiment to which you have given utterance. His exterior is rough, but he is sound at core. You will hardly believe me when I tell you that he lay awake half the night regretting the intemperate language which he used in your presence.

Mrs. S.—And well he might, Mr. Marsden :—well he might. However, I am glad that he is sorry.

M.—And, Mrs. Smart, you must allow me to say that you are unfair towards him. If you knew him better, your opinion of him would be very different. About three o'clock this morning I was awoke by hearing him sigh. I asked him whether he had a touch of liver, or whether the mosquitoes troubled him. 'No, Marsden,' said he, 'I was 'reflecting on my unhappy fortune in having parted in anger 'with a lady whom I so cordially respect as the last existing 'specimen of the good old Anglo-Indian style—'

Mrs. S.—Did he say that?

M.—'That style which went out with the old Company—'

Mrs. S.—Upon my honour!

M.—'A lady who is daughter, sister, and wife of Sudder judges.'

Mrs. S.—Really, now!

M.—'Marsden,' he said, 'how that woman will shine in 'Chowringhee when Smart goes to Calcutta to take his seat 'in the Supreme Council.'

K

Mrs. S.—Poor Mr. Judkins! His head was turned by his appointment to Budgemahal, but his heart is in the right place.

M.—I knew that you would come to think so, Mrs. Smart. But he is coming out of the tent. Pray, Mrs. Smart, receive him with cordiality. He is dreadfully depressed. [*Aside.*] He looks like it.

Enter JUDKINS.

J.—Mrs. Smart, my servants have informed me how scandalously you have been treated by your bearers. I can assure you that the budmashes shall receive their deserts.

Mrs. S.—I have no doubt that everything will be done which justice can demand.

J.—Yes, Mrs. Smart, budmashes have a bad time of it in my division. In 1857 I was the terror of all the disaffected villagers for a hundred miles round. The wives of sepoys used to silence their children with the dreaded name of Judkins. The people of those parts long will tell how, on the information that a mutineer was concealed in a neighbouring jungle, I turned out with my elephants and horses ; how I marched night and day for eleven consecutive hours ; how I surrounded the lair of the fugitive with a cordon of burkundazzes ;* how I advanced into the thicket, accompanied by the slender escort of three thannadars† and a tipsy darogah ;‡ how fiercely I flung myself on my prey—

Mrs. S.—And how you hung him, I suppose, Mr. Judkins?

J.—Well, Mrs. Smart, to tell you the truth, he turned out to be a bunnya,§ who had concealed himself for fear of

* Policemen.   † Sergeants.   ‡ Inspector.
§ Shopkeeper.

the disbanded sepoys. But I trust you and Miss Smart will repose yourselves in my tent while the gharee is getting ready. Breakfast will be on the table in half-an-hour. I should feel highly honoured if you would share our meal.

Mrs. S.—Sir, I shall have the greatest pleasure.

[*Exeunt Mrs.* SMART, FANNY, *and* MAID *into tent*.

M.—Why, Sir, how seductive your manners have become all of a sudden! You have talked over the old lady already. But what is the meaning of all this bobbery? [*Noise heard*.

Enter CHOLMONDELEY, *in the custody of two Bengal police, and followed by a ryot*.

J.—Mr. Cholmondeley! in Heaven's name what has happened? I trust you have not had what the *Hurkaru* calls 'an unfortunate collision with a native:'—a collision in which, somehow or other, the native always comes off the worst.

Ryot.—Hussoor, Sahib ne hamara soor marra hai.*

C.—Upon my honour, Mr. Judkins, I have not the slightest idea what my crime may be. All I know is that my beaters started a fine hog, which I rode down and speared. While I was engaged in cutting off his head as a trophy, this native fellow came up and made a great noise, calling out something about hamara soor, and foujdaree.†

J.—Well! how did you reply?

C.—Why, I said, 'Jungly soor doom,' and held my finger out like that [*crooks his finger*]. On which he said

---

* 'Please your worship, the gentleman has killed my pig.'
† Justice.

'Nahin, Sahib, jungly soor ke doom seder hai.'* [*Straightens his finger*].

J.—And what did you say to that?

C.—Why, I told him to stop his noise, or I would give him a thrashing.

J.—Well, what next?

C.—Why, he called in these two peelers, who happened to be passing, and they brought me here like a condemned felon.

J.—Well, the question is, whether the pig was tame or wild.

C.—Mr. Judkins, I may be a young pig-sticker, but I am too old a sportsman to make such a mistake as that. However, to convince you, I have brought away the tail. [*Holds out a curly tail.*]

J.—My dear Sir, if pigs are tame in proportion to the curliness of their tails, this is the most civilised animal of the sort I ever came across.

C.—But, happily, as pigs are tame in inverse proportion to the curliness of their tails, this must be the wildest hog in all the North-West.

J.—Mr. Cholmondeley, you are under a fatal mistake. Wild pigs have straight tails, and tame pigs curly ones.

C. [*clasps his hands before his face*]—Undone! undone!

J.—Well, Mr. Cholmondeley, you certainly have committed a misdemeanour; but I don't know under what head it comes in the Penal Code. [JUDKINS *takes up the 'Code.'*] I'll look through the index. Let me see. 'Housebreaking 'by night.' Your offence can hardly be said to come under that section. 'Idiot—Act of, when no offence.' But you're

---

* 'No, Sir, a wild pig's tail is like this.'

not an idiot. [*Aside.*] He's only a fool. 'Landmark—
'Diminishing usefulness of one fixed by public servant.'
You certainly have diminished the usefulness of a pig, but
that animal is not a landmark fixed by a public servant.
'Lieutenant-Governor—Assault on.' 'Member of Council—
'Attempt to overawe.' I hope you haven't been attempting
to frighten Mr. Laing into renewing the Income-tax—eh,
Cholmondeley? This looks more like it: 'Mischief—
'Punishment for, when simple. By exhibiting false light or
'mark to mislead navigators.' You have not by any chance
been exhibiting a false light or mark to mislead navigators,
have you? 'By causing inundation or obstructing drainage.'
That won't do. Oh, here it is: 'Whoever commits mischief
'by killing, poisoning, maiming, or rendering useless any
'animal or animals of the value of ten rupees or upwards,
'shall be punished with imprisonment of either description
'for a term which may extend to two years, or five, or both.'
Ho, you! Tumarar soor ke dam kitna hai?*

Ryot.—Eck sou rupea, Sahib.†

J.—There, Cholmondeley, you are liable to imprisonment of either description for a term of two years, or five,
or both. Which will you take? You may as well have
both while you're about it.

C.—O Lord! This is a dreadful business. Mr. Judkins,
for heaven's sake, arrange it somehow. Why did I come
out to this awful country?

J.—Well, I'll try. Atcha, Sahib teen rupea toom ko
dagabuss.‡

---

* 'What is your pig worth?'
† 'One hundred rupees, Sir.'
‡ 'Look here. The Sahib will give you three rupees.'

Ryot.—Nahin, Sahib, dega teen rupea ath anna.*

J.—Here, Cholmondeley, give this fellow three rupees and a half, and he'll say no more about it.

C.—Lord, what influence you local officers have over the natives! [*Pays the money.*] Thank Heaven! I'm out of that.   [*Exeunt natives.*

J.—Now, Marsden, we'll go in to the ladies. Breakfast must be ready by this time. You'll join us soon, I hope, Mr. Cholmondeley.

[*Exeunt* JUDKINS *and* MARSDEN *into tent.*

C.—This unlucky business has quite taken away my appetite for India. I'm hanged if I don't go home by the next boat, and make my arrangements for bringing Sir Charles Wood to book. I'm resolved never to come out here again, not even as Governor-General. Hulloa! There goes that rascal Abdool as drunk as an engine-driver on the East Indian Railway.   [*Exit, calling to* ABDOOL.

Enter JUDKINS *and Mrs.* SMART.

Mrs. S.—Well, Mr. Judkins, I consider that we were very fortunate in having met with our disaster. We have been most magnificently entertained.

J.—You are very good to say so.

Mrs. S.—That vegetable curry was excellent. Of course your cook is a Mug.† What do you give him?

J.—Well, Mrs. Smart, he used to get eighteen, but now I've cut him two rupees. I told him that it would never do for domestic servants to get the same, now that civil servants are being cut all round. Hang these reductions, Mrs.

---

* 'Ah! Sahib, give me three rupees eight annas.'
† A native of Arracan, whence the best cooks come.

Smart! Hang these reductions! The Civil Service will soon cease to be a decent provision for the cadet in the family of a thriving greengrocer.

Mrs. S.—Yes, you and I have lived to see sad changes, Mr. Judkins. I remember the days when every servant in my house was a Government chuprassie,† with the exception of the khansaumaun and a Portuguese ayah. Now we think ourselves well provided if we have some six fellows, who grumble if they are told to carry a chit* or take the children a walk.

J.—Yes, Mrs. Smart, times are altered. Times are altered.

Mrs. S.—They are indeed, Mr. Judkins. But do you know that Mr. Marsden reminds me of the good old style more than any young man whom I have met for years? He has quite the manners of the best set among the junior factors a quarter of a century ago.

J.—Ah, Madam, I wish you could bring yourself to look more kindly on his suit, both for his sake and for Fanny's. It is impossible to avoid seeing that she will never be happy with anyone else.

Mrs. S.—Well, I am not opposed to the marriage on mercenary grounds. He is low down in the Service; but that matters little at his age. A clever Assistant-Magistrate is a better match than a foolish Collector with Full Powers. But, Mr. Judkins, I am a woman of principle. I cannot and will not give my daughter to a man whose appointment is not pucka.

---

* Messengers. In old days these officers were very generally employed for domestic purposes.

† A note.

Enter TROOPER.

Trooper.—Commissioner Sahib ke waste chittee hai. [*Presents a letter*—JUDKINS *reads.*]

J.—Here, Marsden! Fanny! All the world! Come out here, everybody! O yes! O yes! Listen all good people!—' The Lieutenant-Governor, having received in- ' formation that the bridge over the Rotawaddy nullah, built ' by Lieutenant Marsden, of the Bengal Native Infantry, ' Acting-Assistant-Sub-Deputy-Inspector of Bridges in the ' Public Works Department, stood during the whole fort- ' night of the rains, and then only gave way in one arch, ' desires to express his satisfaction in the conduct of that ' officer by confirming his appointment.' Frank, I con- gratulate you. Come, young fellow, go and thank the powerful friend to whom you owe the appointment. There she stands. [*Points to* FANNY.]

M.—I must first request Mrs. Smart to inform me whether the gulf which separates me from her daughter is bridged over as well as the Rotawaddy nullah?

Mrs. S.—Well, Mr. Marsden, you have *now* my leave to say what you like to Fanny.

M.—Fanny, I am cutcha no longer. May I become a covenanted servant in the sweetest sense? [*Kisses her hand.*]

Mrs. S.—Well, it seems that you will not have much difficulty in that quarter.

J.—But what will Mr. Smart say to it?

Mrs. S.—O, pray don't trouble yourselves about that. Mr. Smart does not play the Sudder Judge in his own family. [*Coming forward.*] And now only one thing remains. Whatever may have been the merits of our acting, the per- formance must be cutcha unless *you* confirm it with your applause. Will you pass an order to that effect? As to the stage, scenery, and dresses, we have done our best, and the Lieutenant-Governor his kindest ; and we trust that we may with confidence ask the vital question—'Were the appointments pucka ?' [*Curtain falls.*]

A HOLIDAY AMONG SOME
OLD FRIENDS.

A HOLIDAY AMONG SOME OLD FRIENDS.

OUR own poets have described, far too minutely to need repetition here, the charms and glories of Grecian scenery :—the chains of lofty peaks, their summits crowned with snow, and their lower slopes clad with dwarf-oak and arbutus ;—the valleys running from the shore into the heart of the mountains ;—the bold headlands alternating with shady creeks, the haunt of nymphs in the days of Hesiod, and the lair of pirates in the days of Byron. This fair region is now for the most part deserted and neglected, brown and arid from the disuse of artificial irrigation. The traveller paces across the market-place of Sparta revolver in hand, and with side-long glances into the bushes that fringe his path ; and amidst the ruins of Thebes the sportsman may shoot in a forenoon woodcocks enough to make the fortune of ten Norfolk battues. But it was not so always. There was once another and far different Greece, which can no longer be visited by steamer, and diligence, and railway ; —which can be viewed only through the medium of her own eternal literature. In the old time every one of those valleys swarmed with cattle, and blushed with orchards, and glowed with harvests. Every one of those innumerable creeks was the site of some proud city, whose name, and history, and legendary lore are familiar to the British school-boy long before he can name within fifty miles the locality of one in three among the great seats of industry enfranchised by the bill of Mr. Disraeli.

Each of these cities was a little state in itself, governed by its own laws, its own interests, and its own traditions. It is difficult for the member of a great European nation to realise such a condition of things. These notable communities, whose names have been household words to the educated men of fourscore generations,—Argos and Mycenæ, Corinth and Megara,—were mere parishes compared with the smallest kingdoms of our epoch ;—mere bits of territory, seven, ten, or fifteen miles square, with a walled town planted somewhere towards the centre of the region. Athens was the most populous among the whole cluster of Grecian states, and the Athenian citizens who were capable of bearing arms in the field numbered only sixteen thousand in the days of Pericles. She was by far more opulent than any of her neighbours ; and yet her public revenue at no time reached half a million sterling. And, nevertheless, these tiny republics carried matters with a high hand. They waged war, and despatched embassies, and concluded alliances with a solemnity and an earnestness which would do credit to the government of the most extensive modern empires. They had their Cavours, and their Palmerstons, and their Bismarcks. They swore to treaties of guarantee as readily, and violated those treaties as complacently as any European statesman of our days. One little nationality would invade the confines of another with a host of seven hundred foot and two or three and twenty cavalry ; while the invaded party would retaliate by despatching a fleet of a dozen cock-boats to lay waste the seaboard of the aggressors.

A homely illustration will give a better conception of Grecian international policy than pages of antique statistics. Imagine a jealousy to spring up between the boroughs of the Falkirk district and the boroughs of the Stirling district, in consequence of the authorities of the latter community having assessed to poor-rates the sacred soil of Bannockburn. On a misty drizzling night towards the end of November some burgesses of Linlithgow, who are not satisfied with the result of the late municipal elections, open one of the gates to a party of the enemy. The Stirling men enter the town stealthily, penetrate to the Grassmarket, and then blow a bugle, and invite the citizens of Linlithgow, on pain of sack and massacre, to separate themselves from the neighbouring boroughs. The inhabitants are at first taken by surprise; but presently they recover themselves, and stand on their defence. They overturn waggons, tear up the pavement, man the walls, and send off posthaste for assistance. Down come fifty score stout fellows from Lanark and Airdrie. The invaders make a gallant resistance, but are overpowered and slaughtered to a man. Then the cry for vengeance rises over the whole Stirling district. Hostilities are at once proclaimed. The town council assembles, and passes a war-budget. A duty of five per cent. is laid on butter, and ten per cent. on woollen cloth. There is to be a loan of twenty thousand pounds, and a vote of credit for three thousand five hundred. The local Tories object to this lavish expenditure; upon which two leading Conservatives are banished, and two more are slain in a popular tumult. The Stirling people take into their pay three hundred Perthshire Highlanders, commanded by the Duke of Athol's head forester; but, on the other hand, two companies of the City of Edinburgh Volunteers march out of their own accord to the aid of the men of Falkirk. Presently there is a pitched battle under the walls of Queensferry. Mr. Oliphant breaks the right wing of his opponents, and drives it as far as Dalmeny. But, in another part of the field, the discipline and valour of the Edinburgh contingent carries everything before it. Some of the Stirling men fly to Leith; some take refuge in Queensferry. Their leader, after behaving with more than his wonted courage, is left on the plain for dead. The Inverkeithing detachment is caught between the sea and the foe, and entirely destroyed. The booty is enormous. A Volunteer from the Old Town comes home with seven captives; one of whom he makes his groom, and another his footman; three he employs as day-labourers; the sixth, a graduate of St. Andrew's, he hires out to wealthy families as a daily tutor; while the seventh, who happens to be a Baillie, he ransoms for five hundred pounds, a sea-piece by Stanfield, and ten shares in a limited company. This slight sketch will give a shrewd idea of an old Greek war; indeed, were we to substitute "Thebes" for "Stirling," and "Platæa" for "Linlithgow," it would read like a roughly executed epitome of one of the most interesting passages in Thucydides.

The curse of Hellenic life was the constant fighting. Partly from circumstances, partly from natural inclination, the Greeks formed the most quarrelsome family that has existed since the days of Cain and Abel. Those old republics fell out as readily as Scotch and English borderers in the fifteenth century, and then carried on hostilities with yet more system and pertinacity than the most civilised and Christian of the great modern nations. A remarkable indication of the bellicose propensities of these peppery little states is that, instead of declaring war, they used to declare peace. The instant that a five years' truce or a twenty years' truce between two cities had come to an end the contracting parties were at full liberty to begin driving cattle, and cutting down orchards, and burning crops : thereby evincing their belief in the principle that war was the normal condition of human existence.

A casus belli was never far to seek. Now it was a slight offered by individual members of one community to the patron deity of another : now some time-honoured dispute about boundaries, revived for the occasion beneath the genial influence of local jealousy untempered by the possession of ordnance maps : now a complaint about the harbouring of runaway slaves or the entertainment of political refugees. A standing bone of contention was the protective tendency of ancient commerce : which may be realised by depicting to oneself all the towns on the Humber actuated in their mutual dealings by the spirit that existed between the Spanish and English traders in the reign of Elizabeth, when a Devonshire skipper detected west of the Azores might make his account never to see Lyme or Dartmouth again unless he could turn the tables upon his captors. With such a tariff it may well be believed that informers drove a bouncing trade. The prohibition placed upon the traffic in fruit by the Attic law has been immortalised in the term "sycophant," which has somehow lost its original signification of a custom-house spy.

Then there were the claims of the parent city upon the colony : a fruitful source of discord among an enterprising people, pinched for room at home, who in the space of three centuries covered with thriving settlements the coasts of the Ægean, the Euxine, the Adriatic, and the Ionian seas. These claims, in theory most extensive and peculiarly binding, in practice were generally allowed to lie dormant until their resuscitation seemed likely to afford a pretext for going to war. The longest and most determined struggle recorded in Grecian history arose from a dispute between the mother country and the grandmother as to which had the best right to protect their offspring from the incursion of the surrounding aborigines.

Anybody who has watched during a period of some years the diplomatic relations of English municipalities must have been impressed by the strength and permanence of their corporate patriotism:—how greedily the public opinion of a town will cling to any mark of hereditary superiority over a rival:—with what uneasiness it is brought to recognise such superiority in another:—with what perseverance and eagerness the object of desire is sought, and with what satisfaction obtained, whether it be a separate custom-house, or a fresh batch of magistrates, or an exemption from the restrictions on the transport of live cattle, or the abolition of a toll which goes to pave and light the streets of a privileged neighbour. No one can form a true conception of Hellenic society who for a moment loses sight of the fact that Hellas consisted of an assemblage of boroughs with these sentiments of ambition and self-respect intensified twentyfold; sanctified by religious associations; ennobled by the names of heroes and demigods; dignified by the eloquence of orators like Pericles and the imagination of poets like Æschylus and Pindar; inflamed by the recollection of past insults and injuries; unrestrained by the influence of any central and paramount authority. There is much truth in the picture drawn by Aristophanes in his play of the *Acharnians*, where the principal actor speaks as follows, in a very free translation :—

" I hope the spectators will not take it amiss if I talk a little about public affairs, though I *am* playing burlesque :— for one has a conscience, even in burlesque. And this time Cleon will hardly be able to charge me with vilifying the State in the presence of foreigners, because it is too early in the year for foreigners, and we have the theatre to ourselves.

" Now, you must know that I perfectly abominate the Lacedæmonians, and cordially hope that the next earthquake will bring all their houses about their ears ; for I, as well as others, have had their foragers in my vineyard. But, come now, (for I see none but friends about me), why, after all, are we to lay everything to the door of the Lacedæmonians ? For you will remember that certain of our people :—I do not refer to the country in general : don't mistake me for a moment ; I make no allusion to the country in general :—certain dirty, counterfeit, contemptible scamps were always giving the police notice about Megarian woollens. And if they caught sight of a cucumber, or a leveret, or a sucking-pig, or a head of garlic, or a lump of salt, as a matter of course it came from Megara, and was declared contraband on the spot. But these doings were a trifle, and too much in the ordinary Athenian style to need remark, until some young sparks thought fit to go on a tipsy frolic to Megara, and carry off a woman. Whereupon the Megarians were cut to the soul by the outrage, and made reprisals by running away with two of Aspasia's girls ; and so the Grecian world broke out into war for the sake of a leash of baggages. And then Olympian Pericles, in all his terrors, fell to thundering, and lightening, and shutting our markets against the Megarians,

and bringing in a string of prohibitory laws that ran like
drinking-catches.   And, when the Megarians found themselves dying by slow starvation, they petitioned the Lacedæmonians to get the enactments repealed that had been
passed on behalf of those three hussies.   But we would not
hear of it; and so shields began banging together from one
end of Greece to the other.   'It was all very wrong,' you
will say; but how can you expect other people to be more
patient than yourselves?   Why, if a Lacedæmonian had
chartered a bumboat, and run a cargo of a single blind
puppy into one of your dependencies, would you have sat
quiet at home?   Not you.   Before the day was out, you
would be putting in commission three hundred galleys; and
the dockyards would resound with the planing of oar-blades,
and the driving in of bolts, and the shifting of rowlocks,
and the whistling of boatswains; and the streets would be
alive with paying of bounties, and weighing out of rations,
and marines squabbling, and captains getting elected, and
figure-heads getting gilded, and garlic and olives and onions
getting stuffed into nets, and tins of preserved anchovies,
and garlands, and dancing-girls, and bloody-noses, and black
eyes."

The historical interest of these incessant wars is out of
all proportion to their size.   Indeed, military narratives are
usually attractive in inverse ratio to the number of com-
batants engaged; for, the fewer the actors, the more marked
becomes the personal character of the scene.   The result of
a great modern conflict depends on an immense multitude
of incidents, so interwoven that it is all but impossible to
disentangle them and to credit each with its due import-
ance.   A cursory relation of such a struggle as Magenta or
Sadowa is simply unintelligible.   We cannot comprehend

what caused the failure of the attack on the redoubt, and the partial success of the advance en échelon ; how it was that the right centre found itself compromised about three in the afternoon, and why it should not have experienced that sensation an hour earlier or two hours later. On the other hand, when Mr. Kinglake tells the story so that it can be enjoyed and understood by recognizing the human element in the affair, there is the drawback that it takes longer to read the battle than to fight it. He must be a very idle fellow who could afford time to get through the Leipsic campaign when detailed at the same length as the fight on the Alma :—that is to say, if he could find anybody long-lived enough to write it for him. The Duke of Wellington most happily compared a battle to a London ball. Each person at the breakfast-table next morning can recall certain detached occurrences, and can state generally how the evening went off; but no one pretends to ascertain the precise sequence and connection of all those individual experiences. A Greek combat may be likened to a Christmas quadrille in the servants' hall, in which everybody knows that the cook wore lavender kid gloves, and that the son of the house flirted with the lady's-maid.

And so it is delightful to turn from the elaborate technicalities of contemporary warfare to the simple manœuvres by which Miltiades and Epaminondas won and lost their battles. Commanding, as he did, a small but high-spirited body of militiamen—who were at home the equals of their leader, and while on active service never forgot that he was their fellow-citizen ; who, when they behaved well, fought for the gratification of an old grudge or for the honour and advancement of their native town ; and, when not in tone, were much more afraid of the enemy than of their own officers—a Greek strategist was forced to adapt his tactics quite as much to the temper of his men as to the nature of the locality. He was not even permitted to take their courage for granted, as is the privilege of generals who have to do with regular soldiers ; but was under the necessity of haranguing his army whenever there was a prospect of coming to blows. Athenian military men, trained in their courts of law and their popular assembly, were for the most part voluble enough ; but it must have been a serious addition to the responsibilities of an honest Bœotian veteran to spend the eve of an action in stringing together platitudes about patriotism, and tutelary gods, and ancestral ashes, when he ought to have been eating his supper and visiting his outposts.

A good illustration, both of the minute scale on which a Greek commander conducted his operations, and of the weight which he attached to catching his adversaries when they were not in a fighting humour, is afforded by Cleon's expedition to Amphipolis, against which he marched at the head of 1,500 foot and 300 cavalry. Brasidas, the best partisan leader of the day, and perhaps of all time, hesitated to attack so powerful a force in the open field, and made arrangements for sallying forth upon the invaders at an unexpected moment, just as they should imagine that they were going to occupy the place without opposition. But it so happened that some Athenian scouts espied symptoms of an ambuscade within the city, and took the information to Cleon, who, having reconnoitred the Spartan position by the very primitive method of looking underneath the gate, ordered his column to draw off towards higher ground. Upon which Brasidas said to those about him, "I can see by the movement of their heads and their pikes that the enemy will not stand. People who march in that style never await the onset. Throw open the gates, and let us charge them like men who are sure to win !" And with a hundred and fifty picked soldiers at his heels he ran out to his last victory.

The multifarious talents and accomplishments that were indispensable to a Greek general made a heavy demand even upon the many-sided Athenian character. It was of primary necessity that he should be a skilful diplomatist, in order to keep his network of intrigues under his own hand, and not leave them to the criticism and manipulation of his political rivals at home. He had one agent at the Macedonian court, urging Perdiccas to attack the hostile colonies from the land-side, and promising, in return, to get the heir-apparent naturalised as an Attic freeman ; another among the Thracian mountains, levying a corps of archers and slingers, and doing his best to prejudice the barbarian intellect against the Lacedæmonian recruiting-officers ; while his most confidential emissary was at Sardis, watching the carefully balanced policy of the Satrap, or even posting up-country on a six months' journey to the neighbourhood of the Caspian sea, with a remote hope of inducing the Great King to forget Marathon. He must know the rudiments of divination, so as to keep a sharp eye on his prophets, and insist with authority, when he had once made up his mind to engage the enemy, on the priest sacrificing sheep after sheep until the omens chose to be favourable. He must be well acquainted with naval matters, in a country where nine-tenths of the fighting took place among the islands or along the sea-board. And, besides being something of a soothsayer, and something more of a sailor, it was, above all, essential that he should be very much of

a politician; for the success or failure of a military enterprise was inextricably bound up in the changes and chances
of internal politics.   Throughout the towns of Greece the
oligarchy held staunchly by conservative Sparta; while the
democracy looked to Athens as their natural patron and
protector; regarded her triumphs and humiliations as their
own; summoned her without scruple to the rescue, if their
political adversaries proved too strong for them to manage
single-handed; and, when their own ascendancy had been
secured, freely sent their ships and squadrons to back her
quarrel for the time being.   A member of the popular party
at Corinth virtually reckoned an Athenian as his country-
man, and a Corinthian aristocrat as an alien; whereas a
Megarian tory would far rather see a Lacedæmonian garrison
in the citadel than a liberal majority in the senate.   If
her friends gained the upper hand, a city which had been
a thorn in the side of Athens might in a day become an
outpost for her protection; while a lucky *coup d'état*, or
a few judicious assassinations, might place thousands of
shields and scores of galleys at the disposal of Sparta.   So
that a wise commander paid quite as much attention to the
opinions of the enemy as to his own tactics; and a prudent
engineer trusted less to his scaling-ladders and his mines
than to the chance of finding a gate left on the jar, or a rope
hanging over the parapet.   A general unskilled in statecraft
was about as useful as an electioneering agent who ignores
Church matters.

In every Greek state there existed these two parties,
ranged against each other in open or covert hostility.   The
democratical faction was strong in numbers and enthusiasm.
The oligarchial faction held its own by dint of wealth,
energy, and an excellent organization.   When the popular

spirit was excited by hope, or resentment, or panic, the onward rush of the masses was irresistible ; but at ordinary times the aristocrats, ever on the alert for an opportunity, gradually recovered their lost ground ; just as the Carlton picked up the great majority of the seats which fell vacant during the continuance of Lord Palmerston's Parliament, while Liberal triumphs are for the most part won amidst the heat and turmoil of a general election. Cooped up within the ramparts of a single town, and brought into daily collision throughout all the departments of municipal administration, these factions hated each other with a ferocity which very seldom for long together confined itself to words and looks. Mutual suspicions, mutual injuries, mutual treacheries soon brought about such a state of feeling that men began to believe in the necessity for mutual butchery. Then came riots in the public places, nocturnal murders of the leading demagogues, arson, chance-medley, and every manifestation of rancour and anarchy. Moderate politicians went to the wall, and were lucky if they did not go to the gallows. Men paid to their party-club the allegiance which they refused to their common country, and did not hesitate to call in the aid of the foreign sword, or the servile torch and bludgeon. When matters were at this pass, a civil war was the inevitable issue. The battle would be fought out among the warehouses, the temples, and the wharves of the unhappy city. Victory would at length place the beaten faction beneath the feet of its vindictive rival. Then would follow proscriptions, confiscations, the execution of scores, and the banishment of hundreds. Bad men would take advantage of the general licence to wreak their personal vengeance, and glut their private cupidity. Debtors cancelled their bonds in the blood of the holders ; lovers laid informations against their successful rivals; actors retaliated on the critics who had hissed them off the stage; and philosophers turned the tables upon some unfortunate logician who had refuted their favourite syllogism.

If any one suspects that this account is overcoloured, let him turn to the fourth book of Thucydides, and read what took place in lovely Corfu, on a day in the late autumn, near three-and-twenty centuries back in the depths of time. After the island had been distracted by internal war for the space of many months, it came to pass that the relics of the oligarchy, some three hundred in number, fell into the hands of their opponents; "who," says the historian, " shut up the prisoners in a large building, and then brought them forth, twenty at a time, tied them in a string, and sent them down between two parallel rows of armed men, attended by people with cart-whips, whose business it was to quicken the steps of those who lagged behind; and whoever happened to have a grudge against any of the captives got a cut or stab at him as he passed by. And sixty had been so disposed of before those in the building were aware of what was going on : (for they imagined that their companions were being simply conducted to another place of confinement). But at last some one let them into the secret : and then the poor fellows began to call upon the Athenian admiral, and bade *him* kill them, if it seemed good to him; but they positively refused to leave the building, and swore that no one should enter from the outside as long as they had power to prevent it. And then the populace gave up the idea of forcing the doors, and clambered on to the roof, tore open the ceiling, and pelted the people below with the tiles; while others got bows, and shot down through the aperture. And the men inside kept off the missiles as best they might; but soon they found reason to give themselves up for lost, and one after another they made away with their lives. Some picked up the arrows, and thrust them into their throats; while others twisted themselves halters with strips torn from their clothes, or with the cords of some beds which happened to have been left about. And far into the night (for the sun went down upon the melancholy scene) they continued dying by their own hands, or beneath the shower of darts and brick-bats. And, when day broke, the townspeople piled them in layers on waggons, and took them outside the city."

From such horrors we are effectually preserved by the very different character of our political situation. Wherever party feeling runs high among a fiery and earnest race, there is always a latent possibility of party violence. Half a century has not elapsed since, on the ground where the Free Trade Hall now stands, the county yeomanry slew fourteen of the Manchester reformers. Barely four years ago the Orange carpenters drove the Catholic navvies into the mud of the Belfast docks, as far as men could wade short of stifling, and then fired at leisure upon their helpless foes. But in a country which counts its inhabitants by tens of millions the very size of the community is a sure pro-tection against any fatal excesses. However fierce and eager may be the factions in a particular borough or city, the force of external public opinion, and the overwhelming strength of the central government, will speedily check all dangerous manifestations of political passions. Where Hel-lenic democrats would have called in the Athenian fleet to assist them in getting the better of their adversaries,— where Hellenic aristocrats would have welcomed an in-vasion of Spartans or an insurrection of serfs,—we content ourselves with telegraphing for a few dozen of the county police, or a troop of hussars from the neighbouring assize-town. And so our civic strife is waged,—not with daggers, and clubs, and fire-brands, and fragments of broken pottery, —but with the more pacific artillery of polling-cards, and handbills, and addresses.

The historians of Greece from Xenophon downwards have imitated the people of whom they write, and make a point of ranging themselves under the banners of one or the other of the two leading cities. This spirit of un-compromising partisanship, excusable, and even graceful in a contemporary, writing of the scenes in which he had acted and the men whom he had loved and hated, becomes somewhat absurd when transferred to pages printed in Paternoster Row. For some time previous to the French Revolution Athens had the best of it. Freedom and equality were the order of the day. Liberals of a milder type talked with admiration of Pericles and Aristides; while sterner spirits were all for Harmodius and Aristogiton, and for carrying their daggers in boughs of myrtle, and for irrigating trees of liberty with the blood of tyrants. Then came the great flood of conservative reaction, which penetrated into this singular side-channel, and produced a crop of authors who discovered that the Attic democracy was a fickle and ferocious mob; so godless that it burned the temples of a conquered city, and so superstitious that it flew into a frenzy of rage and terror when an idol was mutilated by a party of midnight roysterers; so inconstant that it deserted Alcibiades, and so fond and besotted that it always stuck to Cleon. This school could see nothing in the Athenian constitution except ballot, universal suffrage, and graduated taxation, bearing lightly on the poor and heavily on the rich and powerful; struck at Charles Fox in the person of Demosthenes, and bespattered Orator Hunt under the guise of Hyperbolus; and loathed the wreath on the brows of an Hellenic demagogue as if it were the white hat of a British radical. For a generation the serried ranks of Mitford and his disciples carried all before them; but a far keener intellect, and an abler though not an impartial pen, has at length turned the balance of war; and it is probable that Englishmen will henceforward in the main take their opinions on Grecian international history from Mr. Grote's exhaustive yet most attractive work.

When we consider that all Hellenic communities sprang from a common stock, worshipped common gods, and spoke a common tongue, it is not surprising that men of the same political faction should have made a common cause throughout the Grecian world. Even among the heterogeneous races included within the circle of modern civilization there are symptoms that an age is approaching when the patriotism of party will displace the patriotism of locality. Increased facility of locomotion and communication is beginning to do the work of a universal language. There is everywhere a great and growing fellow-feeling between those who worship reason and progress, as opposed to the votaries of force and prescription. And it is by the direction which his sympathy takes with reference to affairs abroad that we can test the real instinct of a man more surely than by his professed opinions on matters nearer home. Towards the close of 1865, on the eve of the political *mêlée*, by observing the tone which a member of Parliament adopted with regard to the Jamaica troubles, a shrewd guess might be made at the lobby in which he would be most often found in the course of the coming session. On the other hand, the tirades of the intellectual French press against English reform have opened our eyes as to the liberalism of certain Paris liberals. The Special Correspondent of *The Times* is great on General Butler's proclamation, Fort Lafayette, and the rising inundation of greenbacks. The radical pamphleteer can see nothing but the barbarity of the Confederate guerillas, and the horrors of a Southern prison. The Conservative, ready charged with pity and indignation, waits for the news that Maximilian has been shot; while the Liberal is prepared to be unable to forget who it was that murdered Ortega and his comrades in vindication of the principle of hereditary divine right, imported to a hemisphere where it never existed from a continent where it is no longer wanted. We condemn the tyranny or violence committed in distant countries on behalf of the cause which we have at heart with a shew of displeasure not more genuine than that which we exhibit when our leading supporter canvasses a tenant in a manner too pressing and with too loud a voice, or when humbler allies evince their attachment by mobbing a hostile freeholder. And when the cause wins a signal victory, on however remote a field, we exult as if at the critical hour of noon there had occurred a favourable turn in the tide of a hard-fought contest; as if, to the sound of the workmen's dinner-bell, yards and factories were pouring forth their streams of friendly voters; while already our own statement of the poll places us five hundred to the fore, and our opponent contents himself with a majority of eleven. To the true soldier, as long as the day goes well, it matters not whether the enemy are giving ground on the extreme of the farthest wing, or in his own immediate front. Success is the same, whether gained among the pine-forests of

Virginia, or the vineyards of Lombardy, or on the Bohemian slopes, or around the Westminster hustings.

The security of these little Greek boroughs, hating each other more bitterly than Vienna and Turin, and situated in closer proximity than Putney and Islington, depended absolutely on the natural or artificial strength of their defences. In most cases the citadel, in some the entire town, was planted on the summit of a precipitous rock. Where the site was less advantageous the place was surrounded by battlements of immense height and solidity. If the territory comprised a port anywhere within six or seven miles of the capital, the city was connected with the harbour and the dock by works known technically as "long walls." In time of war a sufficient number of the burghers were told off to man the line of circumvallation. A bell was passed from hand to hand, whose continuous ringing announced that the cordon of sentries was on the alert. Sparta, alone of Hellenic communities, scorned to surround herself with material bulwarks other than the corslets of her soldiers; but, like Paris in 1814, she found reason to repent of this over-confidence when her power had been shaken, and her ascendancy called in question, by the vital defeat of Leuctra.

In the eyes of a Greek the town-wall was the symbol of distinct national existence. The first act of a conqueror who desired to have his prostrate enemies permanently at his mercy was to level the fortifications, and split up the municipality into separate villages. In the case where a modern victor would prohibit a dependent sovereign from increasing his standing army beyond police requirements, Lysander or Agesilaus would have thought it enough to forbid the rebuilding of the ramparts. There is little in ancient narrative more curious than the mixture, so in-

tensely Greek, of heroism with mendacity, whereby Themistocles gained time to fortify Athens in the teeth of Spartan
jealousy and selfishness.   And there is nothing more touching than the passage in which Xenophon relates how Conon
sailed straight from his victory off Cnidus to restore the
walls that had lain in ruins since the sad day when, undone
by her own ambition rather than by the prowess of the foe,
after facing Greece in arms for a generation the imperial
city fell.   To the completion of that design the townsmen
fondly looked for the return of her old supremacy and
ancestral renown by land and sea.   They believed that they
should once more see their home such as they loved to
describe her in conventional, but not unmerited, epithets,—
" the bright, the violet-crowned, the enviable, the famed in
song."   And no wonder ; for he who to-day peruses that
story,—though his patriotism is due elsewhere, and his more
enlightened ideas of right and wrong are shocked at every
turn by the iniquity and cruelty displayed by Athens
during the period of her domination,—can hardly repress
a transient hope, in defiance of his acquaintance with what
is now history, that he is again to read of her as she was
under the rule of Pericles ; willing for the moment to forget
that, however deftly the architect might piece together the
scattered stones, no skill or industry could recall the valour,
the energy, the simple hardihood which urged on the galleys
at Salamis, and cut its way through the stockade at Mycale.

The loftiness of the walls, and the multitude of the
garrison, consisting, as it did, of every able-bodied male in
the population, effectually ensured a Greek city from capture
by escalade.   Besides, it was abundantly proved by the
experience of the Civil War in America to what an extent
militia inside a work fight better than militia in the field.

Nor was it easy for the assailants to proceed by the more tardy method of blockade, which would have necessitated the retention under arms for months together of men who, after the first few days of soldiering, began to fret at being kept from their barns and workshops. In the case of a small town that had made itself exceptionally obnoxious the besiegers sometimes had resort to the plan of running a counter-wall round the entire circuit of the fortifications, which could be readily guarded by successive detachments of themselves and their allies until the place was reduced by famine. Athens, indeed, was enabled by her opulence to keep on foot considerable bodies of troops during protracted and distant campaigns. Throughout the siege of Potidæa her heavy-armed infantry at no time fell below a force of three thousand shields, every man receiving pay at the rate of twenty pence a-day. She spent in all half a million of money upon this operation, which closely resembled the siege of Sebastopol in duration, locality, and climate ; and surpassed it in the misery undergone by the invading army.

In the ranks of that army marched a pikeman conspicuous for courage and eccentricity, with whose description Alcibiades amused a circle of guests over the wine of Agathon the tragic poet,—having already taken a good deal too much of somebody else's. "You must know," said he, "that Socrates and I served together at Potidæa, and belonged to the same mess. And there, whenever, as is so often the case on active service, we ran short of provisions, no one came near him in the power of enduring privation. On the other hand, when we had plenty to eat and drink, he shewed a rare capacity for enjoyment ; and, though he did not care for wine, if put to it he could sit out the whole table; and yet no living man ever saw Socrates the worse for liquor: both of which facts the present company are likely to find out in the course of the evening. And during the depth of the winter, (and a winter in those parts is no trifle,) when all who were off duty kept close at home, and the men on guard turned out in the most extraordinary panoply of wrappers, with their feet stuffed into sheepskins and rolls of felt, this wonderful person went abroad in that old cloak we all know by heart, and trudged barefoot through the ice and snow more freely than his comrades who had taken such precautions against the cold.

"And I remember well that one morning early, as he was going about his business, an idea struck him, and he stood still to examine it. And, when it did not resolve itself to his satisfaction, he would not give it up, but remained standing until noon came, and people began to notice him and to say among themselves: 'Socrates has been standing there since morning, thinking something out.' Eventually a party of Ionians, after their dinner, finding the weather sultry, brought out some bedding and lay down in the open air; keeping an eye on him meanwhile, to see whether he would stand there all night. And they were not disappointed, for he never stirred till daylight, when he saluted the rising sun, and went his way."

"Then, too, you ought to have witnessed his behaviour on the occasion when the army was escaping from the rout of Delium; where I was present in the cavalry, and he in the line of spears. When our people broke and ran he walked away with Laches. And I fell in with them, and bade him keep his heart up, as I would not desert him. Now, as I was in comparative safety on the back of my horse, I could watch the pair at my leisure: and there could be no doubt which was the more cool and collected. For Socrates marched along, as if he were crossing the market-place at home, with his nose cocked up and his eyes busy to the right and left, just as you, Aristophanes, described him in your burlesque, quietly scanning the stream of friends and enemies as it poured by with an air which most un-mistakeably proclaimed to all in the neighbourhood that whoever meddled with him would have cause to regret it. And so he brought himself and his companion safe off the field; for, when a man carries himself in that fashion, the pursuers generally keep their distance, and prefer to go after those who are flying helter-skelter."

As a Greek general had seldom the force to storm a city, or the time to starve it out, he for the most part confined himself to two modes of warfare. He would enter the hostile borders, and select some mountain village planted amidst a network of gorges and torrents, or some sheer rock standing out like an island from the surrounding plain, and occupy it with a party of light troops, horse and foot, under the orders of an active and adroit leader. Or perhaps he would hunt up the evicted inhabitants of some town which had perished by the act of the people whom he was engaged in annoying, and plant them down bodily in the territory of their former persecutors. Among all the calamities of war none came so vividly home to a Greek as the presence of a marauding garrison within his own confines. In national pride he equalled the Spaniard, whose first waking thought is said to be that the Englishman is in Gibraltar. And apart from the disgrace,—apart from the bitter conscious-ness that tributary populations would not long submit to the ascendancy of a state which could not keep the enemy off its own soil,—there were the daily losses by excursions of the foragers into the adjacent country; the expense and trouble of feeding the army of observation which watched the approaches, and maintaining doubled and trebled guards along the city walls; the sleeplessness; the worry; the bad food; the bivouacs in the snow; the wear and tear of horsehoofs amidst the ravines where the fighting lay; the nightly disappearance of slaves, the smartest and most valuable of whom were always the first to be aware that they had an asylum close at hand.   During the Peloponnesian War upwards of twenty thousand runaways emancipated themselves by taking refuge in the Spartan outpost of Decelea; and, owing to the increased exigencies of the war both in town and country, Athens, to quote the words of Thucydides, was brought from the condition of a city to that of a military station.

Or in the late spring, when the crops were still in the ground, the belligerent who was the stronger or the more enterprising would summon all his allies to some convenient rendezvous, and repair thither himself with every available man equipped and provisioned for a campaign of from ten to thirty days.   And then he would cross the frontier, and pour forth a deluge of spoilers over the domain of his unfortunate rival.   Meanwhile, in expectation of the coming storm, the entire rural population of the invaded country would have betaken itself to its strongholds.   If the combatant who was inferior on land had command of the sea, the cattle would have been ferried across to the nearest friendly islands; while the agricultural implements, the jars of wine, the family gods, the furniture, and even the fixtures of the homesteads, would have been packed into carts and transported within the walls of the capital.   Unless the farmer was lucky enough to possess a town residence he made shift to live in a temple or an outhouse, or even to encamp gipsy-fashion along the inside of the rampart.

It is easy to conceive the distress of the half-fed and badly sheltered multitude during these most unwelcome annual gatherings. May and June in the Levant are at best trying months, and must indeed have been intolerable in the over-crowded bylanes of a beleaguered town; especially if the engineers of the aggressor succeeded in diverting the supply of water. Grecian cities, never very rich in sanitary appliances, were under these circumstances peculiarly susceptible to the inroads of disease: and it was in such a plight that Athens first harboured the fearful epidemic immortalized by Thucydides in the simple and striking narrative of an eye-witness and a sufferer, which has afforded matter for imitation in many languages and metres. The impatience of the people inside, tormented by drought and discomfort, and goaded to desperation by the scenes of rapine and wanton destruction which were enacting beneath their very eyes, would inevitably break forth in a cry for instant combat. Forgetting that they had surrendered their land to depredation because, at a time when their judgment could be better trusted, they had deliberately come to the conclusion that the enemy were too much for them in the field, they would assail the authorities with passionate demands for permission to strike a blow in defence of their hearths and holdings. At such a crisis a conscientious prime minister or commander-in-chief had indeed a thankless office: and the more so, should the invaders have been careful to aggravate his difficulties by ostentatiously excepting his property from the general spoliation, and thereby attaching to him a suspicion of treachery and collusion. If the leading man had the character required to withstand,

and the influence to restrain, his more impulsive country-men, (a service which they whom he benefited seldom forgave or forgot,) the enemy after a time would grow tired of plundering other people's crops, and, gorged with booty, would march home to gather in their own.

But things did not always end so peaceably. Unless a recent defeat had cooled the temper of the weaker party the third or fourth day of a foray often witnessed the forces of the two cities drawn out face to face. Free from the smoke of a modern engagement, and the fog and drizzle of a suburban British review, an Hellenic battle must have been a gallant sight. In purple tunics and burnished armour the men stood ten, fifteen, and twenty deep beneath a glittering forest of spear-heads. Those who were well-to-do had no lack of gold about their greaves and breastplates, and were dandified in plumes and sword-belts; while even the poorest citizen wore a helmet fashioned by the exquisite taste of a Greek artificer. It must have been a trial for the nerves of the bravest to stand biting his moustache; humming a bar of the Pæan which he was to sing within the next quarter of an hour; wondering whether his widow would marry again; hoping that the cobbler on his right might not turn tail, or the teacher of gymnastics on his left shove him out of the line; dimly conscious meanwhile that his colonel was exhorting him in a series of well-turned periods to bethink himself of the tomb which covered those who died in Thermopylæ, and the trophy which stood on the beach at Artemisium. And then the signal trumpet sounded; and the music struck up; and the whole array moved forward, steadily at first, but breaking into a run when only a few hundred yards separated the approaching lines. And, as the distance between grew shorter, and the tramp of the enemy mingled with their own, the front-rank men had just time to try and imagine that the countenances of the people opposite looked like flinching and that the notes of their war-chant had begun to falter, and the next second there would be a crash of pikes, and a grating of bucklers, and a clutching of beards; and those who would fain be home again were pushed on by the mass behind, excited at hearing others fighting, and with no steel at its own throat; and, after five minutes of thrusting, and shouting, and fierce straining of foot and knee and shoulder, the less determined or the worse disciplined of the two hosts would learn, by one more cruel experience, the old lesson that life as well as honour is for those who retain their self-respect and their shields.

Romantic as were the incidents of a pitched battle on land, the accompaniments of an ancient sea-fight appear still more diverting to an English reader: for a naval action consisted in driving one against another ships almost as slender in proportion to the number of people whom they carried as the racing-boats built by Messrs. Searle of Oxford. Athens, in her day of greatness, far surpassed all other powers in this branch of warfare. Her valiant and noble bearing during the Persian affairs in the first quarter of the fifth century before Christ, as contrasted with the underhand self-seeking policy of Sparta, gained her the general confidence and esteem, and laid the foundations of her empire, which ere long comprehended most of the islands and maritime cities of the Grecian world. Honourably won, her supremacy was upheld and extended by far more questionable procedures, and soon degenerated into an execrable tyranny. She converted the contingent of galleys due to the national fleet from each of those whom she was still pleased to call her allies into a contribution of money, and in so far contrived to lessen the number of states which kept on foot a war-navy; while with the funds thus obtained she put on the stocks annually from twenty to thirty keels— a supply which enabled her to maintain an average of three hundred ships laid up in ordinary. This department was managed with true republican economy. Mr. Seely's mouth may well water when he reads that the cash balance in the hands of the Chief Constructor of the Athenian Admiralty fell short of seven hundred pounds. The galleys were called by every pretty female name whose etymology contained an allusion to the sea; and, when the list of Nausicaas and Nauphantes had been exhausted, recourse was had to the abstract qualities, "Health," "Foresight," and the like; or to words of happy omen, such as "The Fair Voyage," "The Sovereign," and "The Saviour of the State." The Romans, who took to the water on compulsion, and never could be brought to understand how anybody should prefer to fight on a deck who could get a bit of firm and dry turf, thought masculine appellations quite good enough for vessels which they loved one less than another.

The imperial city prudently monopolized nautical skill by taking care that her petty officers, whose excellence was acknowledged by her rivals with despair and envy, should be one and all of pure Attic blood. There was the master, who superintended the sailing of the vessel when the wind allowed the canvas to be spread; the boatswain, who instructed the rowers, gave them the time with his flute, and picked out men with straight backs and strong loins to handle the heavy sweeps of the upper tier; and the steersman, whose aim it was to avoid the direct shock of the enemy's beak, and by a dexterous manœuvre to strike her amidships or astern, sweep away a bank of oars, break her rudder, or perhaps sink her outright with all hands on board. Her vast resources gave Athens the command of the labour-market, and permitted her to take into pay from every port in Greece crowds of seamen to perform the subordinate duties of the ship. But, though at ordinary times the bulk of the rowers were foreign mercenaries, on occasions of urgent public danger the state summoned all her citizens who were not touched in the wind to help in pulling along her galleys. There is something quaint in the notion that Æschylus and Lysias must have been familiar with those miseries which a college crew know so well, and in all probability prided themselves on a pet salve for raw fingers, or a knowing receipt for training. Aristophanes writes with contempt of sluggards who could not shew an honourable blister earned in their country's cause, and commends one of his characters for placing a soft cushion beneath an old hero who had fought at Salamis.

From the causes enumerated in the preceding paragraphs Athens was always beforehand with her adversaries, and established a vast naval superiority at the commencement of hostilities. At an early period of the Peloponnesian War, Phormio, an old salt of the best Attic school, with a score of ships, went straight into the midst of a fleet of forty-seven triremes, and captured twelve of them after a fight which apparently did not last as many minutes. The result is less marvellous when we learn that the allies arranged their galleys in a circle with prows outwards, like the spokes of a wheel : a formation which the land-breeze blowing down the Corinthian Gulf soon converted into a hopeless medley. While the men were swearing at their neighbours and shoving each other apart with poles, the Athenian admiral bore down on them with his squadron of crack sailors following him in single file.   The Peloponnesians soon appeared again, reinforced to a sum total of seventy-seven vessels, and this time much better commanded.   Phormio, by an act of carelessness, was forced to fight at a disadvantage, lost nine of his ships, and had to run for it.   But, when the action seemed to have been already decided against him, the hindmost of the fugitives, noticing one of the hostile galleys considerably ahead of the main body, dodged round a merchantman which happened to be lying at anchor, and sent the presumptuous foe to the bottom; but not before the Lacedæmonian admiral, who was on board the ill-fated craft, had found time to stab himself with his sword.   Upon this the eleven Athenians recovered their courage, turned on their pursuers, drove before them exactly seven times their own number in ignominious rout, and recaptured all that they had lost, besides taking six of the enemy.

Accommodating themselves as best they might to the overwhelming disparity in fighting power the Spartans adopted the usual course of a belligerent who cannot keep the sea, and freely granted letters of marque among their naval allies.   Elastic Greek consciences soon began to ignore the faint line which separates privateering from piracy; and a Megarian corsair was very indifferent as to whether the fishermen and traders with whom she fell in did or did not own allegiance to Attic rule.   All prisoners, especially those whose dialect and credentials ought to have exempted them from capture, were killed as soon as caught, and hidden away by night among the ravines which ran down to the coast.   The public mind, in a general way not over particular with regard to human life, appears to have considered that this proceeding carried somewhat to excess the principle of dead men telling no tales. Accordingly, when shortly afterwards the Athenians found means to seize some Spartan Commissioners who were passing through a neutral country on their way to the Persian court, the whole party were conducted to Athens, put to death without trial or enquiry, and thrown down a chasm among some rocks, as a solemn reprisal for the outrages committed by the Peloponnesian freebooters : a sure method of anticipating summarily the objections of the international jurists on the other side, who indeed had against them an awkward precedent in the case of the heralds of Darius, whom sixty years back the Lacedæmonian authorities had disposed of in a manner precisely similar, even to the smallest details.

Under such a state of things it may well be believed that there were many disagreeable breaks in the round of duties and pleasures which composed the ordinary life of a Greek citizen. It must have been sad news for a rural proprietor, just as the corn was ripening to his mind, and his lambs had got well through the perils of the cold weather, and the fruit was sufficiently forward to allow of a fair guess at the yield of figs and pomegranates, to hear that Spartan cavalry had been seen cutting grass within a league of the frontier. It must have cost him a pang to abandon his cheerful and wholesome programme of country pursuits ;—the morning inspection of the blood-colt which was to do something at the next Isthmian but one ;—the evening gossip over negus and chestnuts about the latest news from Sicily, and the best receipt for pickling olives ;—the fresh air ;—the early nights ;—the presidency of the local games ;—the observance and affection of his neighbours ;—the presence and favour

of the paternal deities, whom he had but last year propitiated
with a new bronze hearth, and a pair of statuettes from the
hand of Phidias's foreman. To exchange all this for a sojourn
in the hot and dreary city;—where bread, and vinegar,
and charcoal, and all that his farm gave him for the taking,
had to be bought at war-prices;—where the first year he
lodged about among his old schoolfellows, and the second
boarded with the agent who in more prosperous days had
disposed of his wine and oil, until, as time went on, and
peace seemed more remote than ever, he had outstayed his
welcome in every quarter, and was fain to squat beneath a
turret on the battlement, beguiling his involuntary idleness
by speculating whether the pillagers would think it worth
their trouble to cut down the rest of his orchard, and
whether the slave whom he had left in charge was likely to
keep dark about the pear-tree under which his plate was
buried.

Nor was the Athenian who habitually resided in town
without cares and trials of his own. Some winter evening,
perhaps, as he was hurrying out to a dinner-party, curled,
and oiled, and in his best tunic,—conning over the riddles
and the impromptu puns wherewith he intended to astonish
the company,—he would see a crowd gathered round some
bills posted on a statue at a street-corner: and then he
would turn to the slave who trotted behind him with his
napkin, and spoon, and box of scents, and send the boy off
to learn what the matter was: and the young varlet would
return with a grin on his face to say that the Theban
foragers were abroad, and that the generals had put up
a notice designating the burghers who were to turn out and
watch the passes, and that his master's name stood third
upon the list. And the poor fellow would send off an

excuse to his host, and run home to fill his knapsack with bread, and onions, and dried fish; and his wife would stuff wool under his cuirass to keep the cold from his bones; and then he would go, ankle-deep in slush, forth into the misty night,—lucky if his rear-rank man were not some irrepressible metaphysician who would entertain him during the march out with a disquisition on the Pre-existence of the Soul, or the difference between Sense and Sensation.

And it might be that on some fine morning,—or, what was worse, on some morning that was anything but fine,— he would find himself in the thick of a naval fight off some reef notorious for shipwrecks. There he would sit on his leather pad, sea-sick, sore, and terrified; the blade of his oar hitting now against a shattered spar, and now across a floating corpse, as he vainly tried to put on an effective spurt; the man in front of him catching a crab, and the man behind him hitting him in the small of the back at every stroke; the boatswain's flute out of tune, and the whole crew out of time; his attention distracted by observing a hostile galley dashing through the surge with her beak exactly opposite the bench on which he was posted.

Aristophanes has a charming passage contrasting the comforts of peace with the hardships of war. "I am glad," says the farmer, "I am glad to be rid of helmets, and rations of garlic and musty cheese: for I do not love battles: but I *do* love to sit over the fire, drinking with hearty comrades, and burning the driest of the logs, and toasting chick-pease, and setting beech-nuts among the embers, and kissing the Thracian housemaid while my wife is washing herself in the scullery.

"For, when we have got the seed into the ground, and the gods have been pleased to send us a timely rain, nothing is so delightful as to hear a neighbour say : 'Well, Comar-chides, what do you propose to do next? I am for sitting indoors and drinking, while the gods do their duty by the land. So come, wife, toast us three quarts of kidney-beans, and pick out the best of the figs, and let the Syrian wench call in the farm-servants : as this is not weather for dressing the vines, or grubbing in the mud, while the soil is all soaking wet. And let some one fetch me out the thrush and the two finches : and there ought to be a black-pudding in the larder, and four pieces of jugged hare : (unless indeed the cat has made off with them, for I heard her at some mischief last evening :) so let the foot-boy bring us three, and give the fourth to his father. And send to ask Æschinades to let us have some myrtle-boughs : and the messenger on his way had best look in upon Charinades, and see if he will come and drink with us, in honour of the rain with which the gods have blessed our crops.'

"And, at the time of year when the grasshopper is chirping his welcome tune, I dearly love to watch my new Lemnian vines, and notice whether they are as forward as they should be : for I am told they are an early sort. And I like to see the wild fig swelling daily ; and, the moment it is ripe, I put it to my mouth, and eat it, and say, 'Bless the dear Seasons !' And that is the way I grow plump and sleek in the summer, and not by staring at a great god-forsaken brigadier-general, with three bunches of feathers and a flaring red cloak, who is always the first to run away when it comes to real fighting."

Had I the choice of time and place wherein to spend the term of existence, considerations of religion and morality apart, I would without hesitation prefer to be an Athenian in the age of Pericles ; for such a man led a life the plan of which was exquisitely tempered with good sense, refinement, and simplicity. He knew nothing of the passions that agitate the modern votary of fashion, who is for ever jostling amidst an endless throng of competitors towards a common centre. He resided among the friends of his childhood; among people who had watched him, his virtues, and his foibles, from his youth up. He had none of our temptations towards assumption, insolence, and extravagance. It was idle to attempt to impose upon folks who knew his income to a drachma. If he aspired to cut a dash by setting up a second chariot, or treating his guests to Chian wine grown in the year of the earthquake, he was aware that all his father's cronies were shaking their heads, and wondering how long Aristippus, the son of Pasias, would take about going to the crows: (for these ill-omened birds answered to what are called the dogs in English metaphorical natural history). If he happened to be short-sighted when an old schoolfellow passed him in the street, he was aware that, at all the dinner-tables of the evening, men would be wondering how the grand-nephew of Ctesippus the process-server could venture to give himself such high and mighty airs. If he felt any aspirations towards a political career, he would think twice when he saw on the front bench of his audience those very contemporaries on whose backs, a few years before, he had been hoisted three times a week to be flogged for his mistakes in grammar and arithmetic. And so it was that society then had a less constrained and artificial aspect than it has ever worn in times past. Men talked for amusement and instruction, rather than for display. They lived with those whom they liked, not with those whom they feared. Their festivities and social gatherings were not special and extraordinary occasions, but formed an integral part of their everyday existence.   They did not dine an hour and a-half later than was pleasant, and sit up five hours later than was wholesome.   They did not suffer themselves to be hustled upstairs by the ladies of their family a little before midnight to dress for a ball where they would have no space to dance.   They did not get together to settle the affairs of the nation in a badly-ventilated senate-house at an hour when all honest men should be in bed,—at an hour when, if we are to believe certain cynics, all honest men *are* in bed.

The Athenian rose early; and, after performing a very primitive toilette, repaired forthwith to the market-place, to hear the news, to transact his business, and to make his purchases for the day.   If he purposed to entertain his friends in the evening, there was no time to be lost.   By seven in the morning the plumpest of the blackbirds, the whitest of the celery, and the firmest of the great eels from the Theban stewponds would have been bought up; and he would be forced to content himself with a string of lean thrushes, and a cuttle-fish whose freshness might be called in question.   Perhaps, while he was engaged in beating down the purveyor, he might hear behind him a sudden rush of people; and, looking round, would see two Scythian policemen sweeping the square with a rope besmeared with red chalk.   Then he would know that a general assembly was to be held for the dispatch of business, and would hurry off to secure a good place.   And there he would sit, as an old Athenian describes himself, groaning, stretching, yawning, scratching his head, jotting down notes, and wait-ing for the appearance of the President and the committee to open the meeting.   And presently, after a sufficiently long interval, the committee would come bustling in;

treading on each other's toes, jostling for a good place, and trying to look as if it was they who had been kept waiting by the audience : for human nature is materially the same, whether on the platform of Exeter Hall, or round the tribune of the Athenian assembly. And thereupon the crier would proclaim : "Who wishes to speak about the Spartan treaty?" and the call would be for "Pericles": and the prime-minister would rise, with his right hand thrust into his bosom, and something would be said which is still well worth the reading. And, when public business was concluded, after a light breakfast, our citizen would return to his shop or his counting-house until the first hour after noon ; and then he would saunter down to his favourite gymnasium, and thence to his bath : for the old Greek did indeed regard his body as a sacred vessel, which he was bound to keep clean, fair, and fit for use, and would as soon have neglected his daily meal as his daily exercise.

Let us suppose, however, that our friend has sprained his wrist at quoits, or cricked his back while wrestling, and accordingly has determined to substitute an afternoon call for his athletic exercises. On such a call let us take the liberty to accompany him. Or rather let us, by the assistance of Plato, follow Socrates and his friend Hippocrates to the house of Callias, an Athenian person of quality, much given to letters. The purpose of their visit was to have a look at three famous sophists from foreign parts. Protagoras of Abdera, Hippias of Elis, and Prodicus of Ceos. "When we had arrived within the porch," says Socrates, "we stopped there to finish off the discussion of a question which had cropped up in the course of our walk. And I suppose that the porter heard us talking away outside the threshold : which was unfortunate ; as he was

N

already in a bad temper on account of the number of sophists who were about the premises. So when we knocked, he opened the door, and directly he saw us he cried: 'More sophists! eh! Master's not at home,' and slammed the door to. We, however, persevered, and beat the panels vigorously with both hands: upon which he bawled through the keyhole: 'I tell you, master's not at home.' 'But, my good fellow,' said I, 'we don't want your master, and we do not happen to be sophists. We have come to see Protagoras: so just send in our names.' And then he grumbled a good deal, and let us in.

"And, when we were inside, we found Callias and his friends walking about in the corridor, seven a-breast, with Protagoras in the middle. And behind them came a crowd of his disciples, chiefly foreigners, whom the great man drags about in his train from city to city, listening with all their ears to whatever was said. And what amused me most was to observe how carefully these people avoided getting in the way of their master; for, whenever he and the rest of the vanguard came to the end and turned round, his followers parted to right and left, let him pass through, and then wheeled about, and fell into the rear with admirable regularity and discretion.

"And after this I noticed Hippias sitting on a chair in the opposite corridor: and around him were seated on footstools Eryximachus, and Phædrus, and a group of citizens and strangers. And they appeared to be putting questions to Hippias concerning natural science, and the celestial bodies: and he, sitting on his chair, answered them in turn, and cleared up their several difficulties. And Prodicus was occupying a closet, which Callias ordinarily uses as a still-room; but, on this occasion, what with his sophists and their disciples, he was so hard put to it for space, that he had turned out all his stores, and made it into a bed-chamber. So Prodicus was lying there, rolled up in an immense number of blankets and counterpanes; while his hearers had planted themselves on the neighbouring beds. But, without going in, I could not catch the subject of their conversation, though I was very anxious to hear what was said (for I consider Prodicus a wonderfully wise personage), because his voice was so deep that the closet seemed full of an indistinct noise, something between humming and buzzing."

In such a picture there is something mighty refreshing to a denizen of that metropolis where a rout which commences at a quarter to twelve, and embraces a tithe of the Upper Ten Thousand, is conventionally described on the cards of invitation by the epithets "small and early." Such refined simplicity, such homely culture, such easy vigour of intellect, and such familiar play of fancy, have been found nowhere since: for they can exist only in a community that at the same time enjoys a large amount of leisure and of vitality: in such a community as Athens, which was in truth an oligarchy, broad enough to present the symptoms of a democracy, based upon a system of servile labour. The number of the slaves was enormous. In Athens, Corinth, and Ægina, they were to the free householders in the proportion of twenty to one. For the most part they were employed as hinds on their master's estates, or artisans working for their master's benefit. A skilled mechanic might be bought for an average price of sixteen pounds; and the net proceeds of his labour ensured his proprietor some thirty per cent. on the purchase-money. The father of Demosthenes made a hundred and twenty pounds a-year by his thirty-two sword-cutters, and fifty pounds a-year by a score of slaves in the pay of an upholsterer. Large sums were given for accomplishments and personal attractions, and yet larger for honesty and high character. A flute-girl with a pretty face and a good ear would fetch a hundred pounds in any market; but the highest price on record was given, by the very Callias whose acquaintance we made above, for a trustworthy man to act as a viewer in his mines. The rank and file, however, of the miners were the least esteemed, and the worst treated, amongst the slave population. They wrought in chained gangs, and died fast from the effects of the unwholesome atmosphere. The domestic servants were tolerably well off, and by many households were regarded in the light of pets. The first comic man of the Greek stage was generally some impudent, pilfering jackanapes of a Thracian slave; who came on rubbing his back and howling out of all proportion to the severity of a well-merited castigation; making jokes that read more decently in their native Attic than in a translation of modern Billingsgate; and singing snatches of airs which, in their popularity and their servile origin, answered to the Ethiopian melodies of our day.

But there was another and a very different class of bondsmen. Ever and anon during time of war, bleeding from recent wounds, and smeared with the dust and sweat of the lost battle, there filed through the streets of the victorious town long strings of downcast captives, who, the day before, had been flourishing merchants, famous lawyers, masters of science, of arts, and of letters. It was not probable that such men would forget, amidst the petty treats and indulgences of a menial life, the time when they were free citizens and happy fathers of families. Their disaffection and discontent formed a perennial source of weakness and danger to the republic. Fear begat hatred, and hatred cruelty. Measures of precaution grew into measures of repression : and repression soon became another word for wholesale slaughter. In Lacedæmon the government sanctioned a policy of extermination, on the ground that the Helots were in a chronic state of insurrection. Thucydides tells us how the Spartan authorities, during the agony of their great struggle against the supremacy of Athens, were driven to arm their serfs, and employ them on military duties : how two thousand of the stoutest and the most courageous among their number were publicly emancipated with every mark of honour; and how, before the triumphal garlands had withered on their brows, every man of the two thousand had disappeared from the face of the land, and was never again seen, alive or dead. And, in the frequent recurrences of panic, the magistrates would choose out the most active and fierce of the young citizens, and send them forth in various directions, provided with daggers and wallets of food. To and fro they ranged, these bloodhounds of a ruthless tyranny, and slew all the Helots of sulky and dissatisfied appearance whom they met riding about the country, and all who happened, in Spartan opinion, to look as if they would take pleasure in cutting Spartan throats. This duty was considered so painful and degrading, that it obtained the title of the "crypteia," or "secret service"; and the names of those to whom it was entrusted were carefully concealed. Gallant soldiers as they were, they cared not to blazon forth the fact that they had been forced to stoop to the office of executioners. Gentlemen to the heart's core, they did not comment in their dispatches upon the physiognomy of the wretches whom the orders of their superiors required them to destroy.

Hellenic warfare, whether foreign or domestic, might have lost something of its barbarity, if Hellenic society had been more generally pervaded by the milder tendencies of female influence. But, unfortunately, the free married women held a most degraded and insignificant position. The mistress of a family neither dined out with her husband, nor was present at the table when he received his guests. Education and accomplishments were confined entirely to ladies of quite another description. Those well-renowned dames of Corinth, Athens, and Miletus, who, like Aspasia, possessed the talents which qualified them to hold a *salon*, belonged to a class which has long ceased to exercise any ostensible sway over modern politics, though it might with advantage engage somewhat less the attention of modern journalism. The same condition of society may be met with in Bengal, where native gentlemen, disgusted by the frivolous and illiterate gossip of their zenanas, are driven to seek intellectual sympathy in the company of clever and cultivated nautch-girls.

The Spartan girls were brought up amidst the manifold hardships and the severe discipline enjoined by their national lawgiver, whose object it was that in courage and bodily strength the woman should be to the man as the lioness to the lion. And so it came about that in Lacedæmon the softer—or rather the less rugged—sex was treated with a consideration that had very little in common with our notion of chivalry; and which resembled not so much the feelings of the Earl of Surrey towards the fair Geraldine as the respect with which poor Tom Sayers may be supposed to have regarded Nat Langham or the Benicia Boy. With this single exception the Hellenic matrons were incredibly debased in morals, habits, and understanding. I blush—

across a score of intervening centuries I blush—to have
written such ungallant words; but a single sentence may
surely be forgiven when we recollect that, year after year,
an Attic audience witnessed with glee and approbation their
wives and daughters exposed to public derision and contempt. Three of the wittiest among the extravaganzas of
Aristophanes are devoted to the faults and follies of his
countrywomen, whom he was never weary of representing
as drunken, lazy, gluttonous, silly, sly, infinitely coarse in
ideas and in conversation. And, hard as the comedians
were on them, the ladies did not come off much better in
the other branches of literature. The two most eminent
philosophers of Greece both came to the conclusion that
the whole duty of woman was to obey her husband. The
popular tragic writer was of opinion that it would be an
excellent thing for mankind if babies could be born without
the intervention of a mother; and the mass of his com-
patriots shewed pretty clearly the relative estimation wherein
they held the sexes by speaking instinctively, not of "wife
and children," but of "children and wife." Witness the
conduct of Socrates in the supreme hour of his life. When
his friends entered the prison, in the morning whereon he
had been appointed to die, they found him just out of his
bath, and his wife seated by him with a child on her lap.
"And then," to quote the narrative left us by one of their
number, "as soon as she caught sight of us she broke out
into the exclamations which women use on such occasions,
as, 'O Socrates, this is the last time these gentlemen will
ever again talk to you, or you to them.' And he motioned
to Crito, and said,—'Crito, my friend, see that some one
takes this poor thing home.' So Crito's people led her off
bursting with grief; and Socrates, sitting up on the bed,

bent his leg towards him, and rubbed it with his hand where it had been galled by the fetter, and said: 'What a singular thing, my dear dear friends, is that which men name Pleasure! What a wonderful relation it bears towards the sensation which is apparently its opposite!'" And so he went his way out of the world, conversing on matters of far deeper import, in the judgment of those present, than the love or the despair of a woman.

One striking effect of a limited national existence was the intense love of country which was engendered in the Greek mind. The calm, philosophical patriotism of the individual member of a vast European people was faint indeed compared with the flame which glowed in the bosom of an Argive or a Corinthian. Those men loved their country because their happiness, their comfort, their very existence was bound up in her well-being. An inhabitant of the British Isles for the most part feels the misfortunes and the prosperity of Great Britain only through his pocket. He knows that his nation is at war with Burmah or China merely by an increase of one per cent. in the income-tax, or a fall of two per cent. in the consols. If he is curious after such sights, he may perhaps get a look at a captured banner, or at the fireworks which commemorate an honourable peace. If he be of a speculative turn, he may amuse himself with doubting whether the Tower-guns are firing in honour of a victory, or the birthday of one of the younger princesses. But an old Greek knew by very different signs that his country was in danger. Blazing corn-ricks, and smoking villages, and the clouds of dust that marked the track of the hostile cavalry—such were the Reuter's telegrams which told him that the invader was abroad. To this hour it is impossible to read without emotion the great comedian's account—half pathetic, half ludicrous—of the sufferings endured by the Athenian farmer in time of war: how, after the incursion was over, the poor fellow would go back to his holding, and find the olive-trees hewed down, and the vines burnt, and the wine-casks started into the oil vat, and the pigs with their throats cut, and the well choked with rubbish, and a big stone jammed into the works of the trough were he mixed his dough. It is not difficult to imagine the feelings of the honest man the next time he found himself face to face with the people who had done him such a mischief: the eagerness with which he would await the signal of battle; the zest with which he would charge home when the trumpet blew; and the very poor chance a Spartan or Theban would run whose life depended on his forbearance. Victory, to an old Greek, meant personal security, wealth of captives and booty, and a fat slice of the conquered territory. Defeat meant ruin and shame : it meant the burning of his roof-tree, and the slaughter of his cattle, and the running away of his slaves, and the selling of his pet daughter to grace the harem of a Persian satrap. No wonder that he was a patriot in a sense that an inhabitant of London or Paris would be at some loss to appreciate.

And so it befell that, when the hour of trial came, these men gave an example of courage and self-devotion, the memory of which will never perish. Two several times Grecian civilization, which contained the germs of all subsequent European culture and progress, was within a hair's breadth of being swept away by the flood of Oriental barbarism. On both occasions that flood was stayed by the superhuman efforts of Grecian self-sacrifice. In the year 490 before Christ an innumerable host of Persians landed on Athenian soil :—Persians, who had found nothing that could resist the terror of their name from the Indus to the Ægean Sea. The crisis was awful. The states of Greece stood aloof in fear and amazement. Sparta, by an unworthy subterfuge, excused herself from coming to the aid of Athens. But the threatened city was true to herself. Her able-bodied sons turned out to a man, and marched quietly forth to make appeal to the God of battles. Shop-keepers and mechanics, artists, merchants, and farmers, they took down their spears and shields, pocketed their biscuit and salt fish, kissed their children, and walked through their doors without any notion that they were going to take part in an affair which all coming generations would re-member with gratitude and admiration. And, when they came to the sacred Plain of Marathon, they did not stop to count the odds; but went at a run straight into the midst of the twenty myriads of Medes and Phœnicians. Out of breath, but not of heart,—with such line as they could keep, and with so much martial science as a city militia might recall in the heat of contest,—they fought foot to foot and beard to beard, until the conquerors of the world broke and fled. And that very night they marched home to their supper ;—all save one hundred and ninety-two, who were lying, with clenched teeth, and knit brows, and wounds all in the front, on the threshold of their dear country, where it becomes brave men to lie.

And again, after an interval of ten years, the invader re-turned in such force that historians differ as to the number of millions whom he brought with him. He bridged the salt sea, and he cut through the dry land. His army drank up streams, and in a day devoured the substance of wealthy cities. Straight on Athens he marched, offering her vast power and privilege on condition of her agreeing to his terms : and threatening her with fire and sword if she remained obstinate. Again the rest of Greece turned recreant. Bœotia joined the banner of Xerxes. The states of the Peloponnesus consulted their own security : but Athens— deserted, slighted, and betrayed—thought only of the common weal. Themistocles enjoined his countrymen to give up their city to destruction, place their women and children in sanctuary among the neighbouring islands, and take themselves on board their fleet. They obeyed his injunctions. Sorrowful but resolute they left their beloved homes to the spoiler ; for they knew, to quote the words of their own historian, that men constitute a city, and not houses, nor temples, nor ramparts bare of defenders. And, ere long, in the Straits of Salamis, was fought that great seafight which rolled back the tide of Asiatic conquest, and saved the arts, the laws, and the sciences of the West from wholesale and irremediable extinction.

But there is a dark side to the picture of Hellenic patriotism. A Greek readily allowed that he owed his mother-country everything ; but his sense of duty stopped there. In his dealings with foreign nations he had no idea whatsoever of honour, forbearance, humanity, or justice. He spoke no language save his own. He did not profess any consideration for mankind in general, and most assuredly he did not practise such unless it happened to suit his individual interests. There is something most revolting in the extreme ferocity of ancient warfare. Throughout the histories of Xenophon and Thucydides mention is seldom or never made of the wounded in the beaten army. A soldier in the front rank who had lost his shield or helmet,—a fugitive who had once been trampled down in the mêlée,—knew in a moment that he was a dead man. And not only did the belligerents lose sight of compassion. They rarely consulted the dictates of the most common honesty. It is strange to read how these refined and highly educated people coolly cut the throats of garrisons who had surrendered on promise of life : how they voted the extermination of all the males over the age of sixteen in a town with which, a twelvemonth before, they had been bound by the closest ties of social and commercial life. During the Peloponnesian War the little city of Platæa, after a prolonged resistance, was given up to the Lacedæmonians on condition that each of the defenders should have a fair trial. The Spartan notion of giving their enemies a fair trial consisted in asking them whether they had done any service to the Spartan cause during the war : a question which was, of course, a cruel and insulting pre-liminary to murder. In preference to such a court-martial one would almost elect to be tried by two lieutenants of gun-boats, and an ensign who had been gazetted on the previous January.

It is impossible to read the story of the late American war without being conscious at every turn that the de-mocratic patriotism of all ages is the same in its leading features. In intelligent valour, in elasticity of temper, in versatility, energy, and enterprise, there was much in com-mon between the Athenian militia and the citizen warriors who marched under Sherman and Grant. Our professional soldiers are too apt to ignore these qualities (which are the peculiar excellences of an army of free men fighting for an object which they appreciate), and were for ever dwelling upon that impatience of discipline, and those occasional manifestations of unsteadiness in the field, which were at

least as noticeable at Delium and Chæronea as at Chancel-
lorsville and Chicamauga.   And, if the heroes of Plutarch
fought better than the undisciplined levies who behaved as
raw troops always did and will behave at Bull Run and
Ball's Bluff—at any rate no free Greek city, save Sparta in
her best days, ever sent forth a force which could match the
armies of the Potomac and the Tennessee in the years 1864
and 1865.   Laconic in every sense was the answer of the
officer detached to hold the Allatoona Pass against all
comers, who, when he had been surrounded by vastly
superior numbers, replied to the conventional summons
to spare the needless effusion of blood by quietly observing that he was ready for the needless effusion of
blood whenever it should suit the Confederate general :—
gallant words which he did not fail to make good.   And
Leonidas and his countrymen, performing their national
toilette in preparation for the death which they knew to be
inevitable, find a parallel among those veterans in Meade's
army who, when their division was ordered upon a desperate
service, were observed to be silently writing their names
upon slips of paper and pinning them to the breasts of their
blouses.

Nor did these modern republicans fall short of the
Greeks in their performance of the last offices towards those
who had fallen in war.   From every corner of that vast
battle-field, stretching over eighteen hundred miles from
Maryland to farthest Texas, the railways brought back the
embalmed bodies of their slain to the farmsteads of Ver-
mont and Illinois.   Then, too, were heard once more, in
unconscious imitation of old Athenian custom, panegyrics
pronounced over the honoured dead by chosen orators in
solemn assembly of the people.   Such was the speech of

Mr. Lincoln at the consecration of the cemetery at Gettysburg—a speech conceived in the spirit of what is perhaps the most touching passage of the funeral oration in the second book of Thucydides.

"We have come," he said, "to dedicate a portion of this field as a final resting-place for those who here gave their lives that this nation might live. It is altogether fitting and proper that we should do this. But, in a larger sense, we cannot dedicate—we cannot consecrate—we cannot hallow this ground. The brave men, living and dead, who struggled here, have consecrated it far above our poor power to add or detract. The world will little note, nor long remember, what we say here—but it can never forget what they did here. It is rather for us, the living, to be dedicated here to the unfinished work which they who fought here have thus far so nobly advanced, and from these honoured dead to take increased devotion to that cause for which they gave the last full measure of devotion. We here highly resolve that these dead shall not have died in vain; that this nation, under God, shall have a new birth of freedom; and that government of the people, by the people, for the people, shall not perish from the earth."

But the most notable of all the memorial literature, prose or verse, which the occasion produced, was the ode recited at the commemoration of the Harvard University which fell in the July immediately following the close of the war by James Russell Lowell, himself a professor at that institution. The circumstances were in themselves a poem. Ninety-five graduates and undergraduates, most of them quite young men, had perished in the course of the past four years. Twenty-six had died of fatigue, exposure, and camp epidemics, and sixty-nine by the enemy's fire. Hitherto known

on our side of the water by productions in which his muse
wears a comic mask, the poet here adopts that tone of
grave and elevated simplicity which is the essence of lyric
majesty :—

> We sit here in the Promised Land
> That flows with Freedom's honey and milk ;
> But 'twas they won it, sword in hand,
> Making the nettle danger soft for us as silk.
> We welcome back our bravest and our best ;
> Ah me ! not all ! some come not with the rest
> Who went forth brave and bright as any here !
> I strive to mix some gladness with my strain,
> > But the sad strings complain,
> > And will not please the ear.
> I sweep them for a Pæan, but they wane
> > Again and yet again
> Into a dirge, and die away in pain.
> In these brave ranks I only see the gaps,
> Thinking of dear ones whom the dumb turf wraps,
> Dark to the triumph which they died to gain.
> > Fitlier may others greet the living.
> > For me the past is unforgiving.
> > > I with uncovered head
> > > Salute the sacred dead,
> Who went, and who return not.—Say not so !
> 'Tis not the grapes of Canaan that repay,
> But the high faith that failed not by the way.
> Virtue treads paths that end not in the grave ;
> No ban of endless night exiles the brave ;
> > And to the saner mind
> We rather seem the dead that stayed behind.

Blow, trumpets, all your exultations blow !
For never shall their aureoled presence lack.
I see them muster in a gleaming row,
With ever-youthful brows that nobler show.
We find in our dull road their shining track.
     In every nobler mood
We feel the orient of their spirit glow,
Part of our life's unalterable good,
   Of all our saintlier aspiration.
    They come transfigured back
Secure from change in their high-hearted ways,
Beautiful evermore, and with the rays
   Of morn on their white Shields of Expectation !

These sentiments recall to mind the expressions used by Pericles when speaking of the Athenians who fell in the Samian war: "They are like the Immortal Gods: for the Gods themselves are not visible to us ; but from the honours they receive and the blessings they bestow we conclude that they are immortal : and so it is with those who have died for their country."

The memorial volumes to which Lowell's ode forms a fit preface present a very different picture of the part played by New England and the Western States from that which some of our contemporaries thought fit to sketch for their own contemplation. There, in the first pages, we may read how James Wadsworth, one of the most influential of Northern country gentlemen, at the age of fifty-four abandoned comfort, and position, and domestic ties, and fought through all the great Virginian battles, until, in the crisis of the terrible conflict of the Wilderness, at the head of his shattered division he threw himself across Long-

street's victorious path. At last his people gave way, and
went back without him. He was found by a Confederate
officer "in the woods, fifteen paces to the left of the Plank
Road. None of the Federal dead or wounded were more
than twenty or thirty yards nearer than he was to the open
field, towards which the attack had been directed. He was
lying upon his back under a shelter-tent, which was extended over him at about three feet from the ground, the
two upper corners being attached to boughs of trees, and
the lower ones and the sides supported by muskets. The
officer recognised him by a paper with his name on it, which
had been pinned to his coat. His appearance was perfectly
natural, and his left hand grasped the stock of one of the
supporting muskets near the ground. His fingers played
with the trigger, and he occasionally pushed the piece from
him as far as he could reach, still grasping it in his hand.
Supposing he might wish to send some message to his
family the officer addressed him. The general, however,
paid no attention to the words, and it was soon evident
that he was unconscious of what was passing around him,
although the expression of his face was calm and natural,
and his eyes indicated intelligence. It was in this state that
he was taken to one of the Confederate hospitals. No
medical skill could save his life. He lingered from Friday
until Sunday morning, the 8th of May."

We may read, too, of men weakly, poor, and some
already elderly, who went into the ranks as common soldiers,
at the call of conscience, and not of glory. Take, for instance, Daniel Hack, who "graduated in 1856, having at
the time the intention of studying law. He did not, however, carry out this intention, but connected himself with
the printing business of his father in Taunton, and there

remained till January, 1864, when he enlisted in the Fourteenth Massachusetts Battery. He remained in camp at Readville about four weeks, and was detailed as a clerk at head-quarters. At a review of troops by Major-General Burnside he stood for several hours with wet feet, and, being physically delicate, contracted a severe cold, which brought on congestion of the lungs. He went home on a furlough of three days, which was afterwards, on his continued illness, extended to three weeks. At the end of that time he returned to camp, but was dropped, during that month, for physical disability, without having been mustered into the service.

" Persevering in his efforts to join the army he went to Hartford, Connecticut, and enlisted as a private during the same month, but was again taken ill before being assigned to any regiment, and died at Hartford, April 17, 1864, aged twenty-nine years. His friends were with him in his last illness, and bore his body home for burial.

" Thus died, after two enlistments within two months, both times as a private soldier, and the second time with the hand of death almost visibly upon him, a young man who was scarcely known even to his classmates, and who was yet endeared to those who knew him by many amiable qualities. He died without seeing a battle-field. His name hardly appears upon the military records of his country, but he gave her all he had to give—even his life."

Later in the book, when the births begin to date no earlier than the forties, we come upon lads of the type that our universities know so well; deep in Plato, and Emerson, and Carlyle; for ever discussing the comparative merits of the life of action and the life of contemplation; pining after an ideal, and finding it, where once they little expected, in a brief career of hardship and peril; going home to Boston or Philadelphia to be cured of their wounds, like schoolboys returning for the holidays, until, after some murderous day, instead of the son or brother, there came a letter from the commanding officer, accompanied by a sword, or a watch, or a pocket-book scribbled over with the familiar hand-writing. Such was Charles Russell Lowell, one of Sheridan's ablest cavalry colonels, at nineteen much given to mysticism and transcendentalism; at nine-and-twenty, in the moment of victory, shot through neck and lung on the back of his fourteenth charger. Such were Robert Gould Shaw and his fellows, steadfastly facing the scorn and ridicule bestowed on all who served with black regiments; cheerfully submitting to the prospect of meeting with neither quarter nor Christian burial, and being huddled into a trench along with their dead negroes :—a shameful grave in the estimation of a Southern planter, but one where a brave man may rest as peacefully as in a village churchyard, and as nobly as beneath the aisle of a proud and ancient minster. And to think that the very existence of these men—our equals in birth, circumstances, and education—happier than us in that they possessed a cause for which they had a right to labour and to suffer—was successfully concealed from us home-staying youth! That we were almost brought to believe that a nation composed of high-souled descendants from the loyal chivalry of the seventeenth century had been subjugated by a heterogeneous mob of aliens officered by political jobbers !

> " Who now shall sneer ?
> Who dare again to say we trace
> Our lines to a plebeian race ?
> Roundhead and Cavalier !

Dreams are those names erewhile in battle loud.
Forceless as is the shadow of a cloud
    They live but in the ear.
That is best blood that hath most iron in't
To edge resolve with, pouring without stint
    For what makes manhood dear."

THE END.

CAMBRIDGE :— PRINTED BY J. PALMER.